DANGEROUS
SPIRITS

OTHER BOOKS FROM JORDAN L. HAWK:

Hainted

<u>Whyborne & Griffin:</u>
Widdershins
Threshold
Stormhaven
Necropolis
Bloodline
Hoarfrost

<u>SPECTR</u>
Hunter of Demons
Master of Ghouls
Reaper of Souls
Eater of Lives
Destroyer of Worlds
Summoner of Storms
Mocker of Ravens

<u>Short stories:</u>
Heart of the Dragon
After the Fall (in the *Allegories of the Tarot* anthology)
Eidolon (A Whyborne & Griffin short story)
Remnant, written with KJ Charles (A Whyborne & Griffin / Secret Casebook of Simon Feximal story)
Carousel (A Whyborne & Griffin short story)

DANGEROUS SPIRITS

Spirits Book 2

JORDAN L. HAWK

CHAPTER 1

"**AND THAT** is my report," Henry Strauss concluded. "We successfully put an end to the haunting, and the usefulness of my inventions was proven once and for all."

He stepped away from the podium where he'd placed his notes and gazed out over the gathering. Almost every member of the Baltimore Psychical Society had come to hear his lecture, and he scanned the faces of the men—and a few women—awaiting the spread of approving smiles. The beginnings of applause. Perhaps a standing ovation?

The small lecture hall remained utterly silent, save for the occasional cough or rattle of papers. Stony faces stared back at him, and two of the women leaned together, whispering behind their fans.

"Er..." Henry resisted the impulse to tug at his collar. Although the windows were open to let in a breeze, the inescapable heat of early July remained oppressive even after sunset. "Are there, ah, any questions?"

Dr. Kelly, the Psychical Society's president, slowly folded his arms over his chest. His beard jutted out in front of him, like an angry badger attached to his chin. "Mr. Strauss," he said, and Henry tried not to flinch at his cold tone, "for years you have insisted on expounding your wild theories to us. You have claimed our beloved dead are nothing more than electromagnetic aberrations—"

"Because they are," Henry objected. "Otherworldly spirits do manifest as electromagnetic fields, at least on this side of the veil. But our brains themselves are powered by just such impulses. There is nothing wrong with accepting the findings of science."

"These are the souls of the departed! Not mere—mere electrical impulses!" Dr. Kelly glared at him. "I granted you one more opportunity to speak to us, in the hope you might have something useful to say. And you bring us this?"

"Er...yes?" Henry's knees turned to water. He wanted to sink through the floor. Or hide behind the podium, perhaps, until everyone left. "I...I thought my inventions made a very good showing."

Kelly dropped his arms to his sides, his face thunderous. "A good showing? Mr. Gladfield, the very man who invited you to try your inventions, *died,* Mr. Strauss! I'm sure I have no need to remind you he was a close friend of this society's former president."

"Well, yes." Henry's thoughts scrambled wildly, like rabbits in a trap. "But—"

"Not only did this haunting end in utter disaster, the owner of the house dead and yourself almost killed by a maniac, but you still had to rely on the actions of mediums to remove the spirits."

"But we did remove them!" Henry seized on the fact. "By combining the best of our abilities, Mr. Night and I put an end to the haunting and freed Reyhome Castle's trapped spirits."

"It seems to me," said Mr. Tilling, the secretary, "your presence rather made things worse. If Mr. Gladfield hadn't made the thing into a contest and involved you, a group of competent mediums would have cleared the house without such...mayhem."

Henry swallowed. "I-I don't wish to speak ill of the dead, but if Mr. Gladfield told us beforehand what to expect, things might not have—"

"Don't blame Mr. Gladfield for your failure," Kelly cut him off. "I suggest you retire to your store and ask yourself if you might be better suited to another line of work. And I will thank you not to darken the doorstep of this society with your presence again."

He rose to his feet and departed with swift strides. The rest of the society took its cue from him, shuffling toward the exit, collecting capes and hats along the way. A few shot Henry amused looks, others sly sneers as they exchanged remarks with their friends. Thankfully the scuff of shoes and rustle of clothing kept him from making out their words.

Henry's face burned with humiliation, and his fingers shook. He wanted to flee, but there was nowhere to go. So he only stood on the stage, until everyone had left except for one other man.

"I'm sorry, old boy," Arthur Burwell said as he made his way to the stage. His steps echoed in the otherwise empty room, magnified by the acoustics. "Dr. Kelly is an ass, to have said such things in front of everyone else."

Henry looked at Arthur, the only person who'd stuck by him after the Strauss family fell from respectable wealth to impoverishment. He'd stood at Henry's side since boyhood, through all the years of striving and setbacks.

For the first time, Henry wished his friend absent. Thank heavens neither Vincent nor Lizzie possessed any interest in joining the Society, and thus missed the debacle.

Henry swallowed again; his collar seemed intent on strangling him. "I...I thought they'd finally see. Now that I have proof..." He trailed away as Kelly's accusations came back. "You don't think he was right, do you? Was I responsible for Gladfield's death?"

"No, of course not," Arthur said staunchly.

Arthur didn't know the details, though. If Henry hadn't exposed Lizzie's secret—that the anatomy beneath her petticoats wasn't what one might expect—Gladfield wouldn't have attacked her. The swirl of pain and fury wouldn't have given the ghost the energy to hurl Gladfield over the balcony and to his doom.

"Clearly Mr. Night and Miss Devereaux believe in your work," Arthur went on. "They wouldn't have gone into business with you otherwise, would they?"

"I suppose not." Still, Kelly's words seemed to ring in his ears.

With a sigh, Henry gathered his papers from the podium. How proud he'd been of the presentation. He'd worked on it for weeks, performing it in front of a little audience of Jo, Arthur, Vincent, and Lizzie. Jo clapped when he finished, her face bright, so proud of her cousin. And Vincent—they'd joked about Henry having to go on tour, or being invited to take over the presidency of the Psychical Society.

Oh God. "Vincent. I'm supposed to meet him at the saloon."

Arthur nodded solemnly. "A good thing. I imagine you could use a drink."

Henry stood outside the saloon and tried to dredge up a smile. He wished for Arthur's strong shoulder to lean on, but his friend had a wife and young child, to whom he returned immediately after the lecture.

Vincent had suggested they meet here to celebrate Henry's triumph. Tonight, after all these years, the Psychical Society was to have finally given Henry his due. They were meant to toast Henry's victory with whiskey, laugh and sing until the barkeep threw them out, then stumble home to bed and a more private celebration.

Instead, he'd have to go in and confess the humiliating truth.

He took a deep breath, fighting against the hollow ache in his chest. Vincent would be outraged on Henry's behalf when he found out, surely. As Arthur said, he'd seen the usefulness of Henry's inventions, believed in them so much he agreed to go into business together. Moreover, to talk Lizzie into doing the same, uprooting them both from New York to Baltimore in the process.

In other words, Vincent had bet his entire livelihood on Henry's ability to make his inventions acceptable—marketable, even. And Henry couldn't even convince the Psychical Society they were anything but a hazard. What hope did he have of convincing other mediums, or the general public?

Perhaps Dr. Kelly was right. Perhaps he should give up on the spirit world and turn his attention to more practical pursuits. But it would mean admitting Vincent had wasted both his time and his money on Henry's schemes. What could he say? *"Sorry you and Lizzie poured every cent you own into our shop. Better luck next time?"*

The situation hadn't come to that yet. Perhaps it wouldn't. Henry would simply worry about getting through the next few minutes and gauge Vincent's reaction afterward. Taking a deep breath, he squared his shoulders and pushed open the door.

Laughter and the clink of glasses greeted him. The saloon was a comfortable place, full of polished wood and brass, and he'd drank here many a time with Arthur. Sometimes when he needed encouragement or a friendly ear, sometimes to celebrate—his scraping together enough funds to buy his repair shop; Arthur's engagement; the opening of the new occult store with Vincent and Lizzie. Tonight was supposed to have been another one of those bright memories to cherish long after the final pint was drained.

Henry squinted through the haze of cigar smoke in hopes of spotting Vincent. He wasn't at the bar, or any of the tables near the front door. Where…?

There. Vincent sat in a far corner, and even after half a year, the sight of him stole Henry's breath. Some would dismiss him for his copper skin, but Henry had always found Vincent achingly beautiful. He'd grown out his thick black hair, adopting the style flaunted by Mr. Wilde during his recent American tour. It seemed to emphasize Vincent's eyes, so dark it was almost impossible to distinguish between pupil and iris. High cheekbones, a wide nose, and full lips completed the picture, but it was the heart within that had truly captured Henry.

And right now, Vincent sat with another man.

Henry recognized the pale hair and skin, coupled with a cream linen coat, even without seeing the man's face. Christopher Maillard, self-styled poet and artist, and handsome as the very devil. A man of independent means with a keen interest in spiritualism and a disdain for the Psychical Society as being too skeptical.

Henry crossed the room quickly. "What do you think of my verse?" Christopher asked Vincent. "Your performance at the séance last month inspired me."

What on earth did he mean? Of course Vincent did private séances, as did Lizzie. But what sort of *performance* would inspire Maillard to capture it in rhyme?

Vincent offered Maillard a lazy smile. "Exquisite work, Christopher. As always."

Henry clenched his fists. Was this to be the cap on his night? To stand here in defeat and shame, while his lover was seduced away by some—some *poet?*

Vincent's black eyes shifted from Christopher, perhaps alerted by some movement of Henry's. A spark seemed to light their depths, and his smile slid from lazy to welcoming. "Henry! You're here at last! I expect all your admirers kept you late with their questions?"

Henry opened his mouth to confess his own heavy feet caused his delay. Combined with the desire not to spend his funds on a cab, as they might have to soon tighten their belts.

"Yes, do tell us all about your lecture," Maillard put in. "I've heard nothing else from Vincent all night. He's positively bursting with pride."

Maillard gave him a look of droll amusement, as if he couldn't imagine Henry having anything interesting or important to say. Vincent gazed at him hopefully. Waiting to hear how all his faith in Henry was repaid.

Without conscious decision, Henry said, "It was a resounding success. The president himself wished to offer his congratulations. I'm sorry to have made you wait."

Vincent threw back his head and let out a laugh of sheer delight. "I knew it! Barkeep! Another round for the table—your best whiskey!"

The smirk slipped from Maillard's face. "Well done," he muttered.

"I…yes," Henry said faintly. And downed his whiskey in a single gulp.

~ * ~

Vincent linked arms with Henry, and they walked—or perhaps stumbled—through the streets back to the shop. Although Vincent rented an apartment of his own, he frequently spent the night in Henry's bed above *Strauss, Night & Devereaux: Occult Services*. Given the lateness of the hour, Jo ought to be asleep by now. Henry certainly hoped so, not because she didn't understand the nature of his relationship with Vincent, but because he didn't want to spin another false tale of the evening.

Why on earth did he make such a statement? And why hadn't he corrected himself immediately?

Vincent had been so proud of him, though. And to confess he'd failed in front of Maillard, to admit Vincent made a mistake when it came to joining his fate with Henry's…seemed unendurable.

"I wore the cufflinks you gave me for my birthday, to bring you luck tonight," Vincent said, holding up his free arm. The small gold stud gleamed faintly in the gaslight. "See? It worked."

"I see," Henry said weakly. He needed to confess the lie. Now, before it was too late.

"Look there!" Vincent exclaimed, swinging Henry around. Startled by the sudden move, Henry nearly lost his footing. Vincent caught him, laughing. "How much whiskey did you have?"

"Not enough," Henry muttered.

"Good." Vincent's eyes took on a new heat. "Because I have another celebration in mind."

Desire tightened Henry's throat—and his trousers. He ached to pull Vincent close and kiss him. But ending the night in jail, on charges of unnatural acts, would take the evening from humiliating to disastrous.

"Don't say such things on the street," he cautioned.

Vincent gestured. "It's after midnight. We're the only fools about. Now look."

Vincent's object of fascination seemed to be an advertisement, pasted to the side of the nearest building.

One Week Only!
Dr. Calgori
Oracle of the Spirits
Will Astound and Amaze You!
Learn the Insights of the Otherworld!

And in smaller print:

This lyceum sponsored by the Baltimore Psychical Society.

Vincent leaned his head against Henry's shoulder. "That's going to be us, someday," he said dreamily. "Up on a stage together. Performing for crowds in New York. San Francisco. London."

Bile clawed at Henry's throat, as if the whiskeys wished to return the way they'd come. He swallowed hard. "Is that what you want?"

Vincent seemed to consider. "I never thought about it before. It would have seemed an impossible dream." He turned his warm smile on Henry. "But with you...everything seems possible."

Vincent had barely shut the door behind them before Henry pounced. Henry and his cousin Jo lived in the small suite of rooms above the shop, while Vincent and Lizzie each leased apartments a short distance away. Henry occasionally spent the night in Vincent's bed, but as he disliked leaving Jo alone for too long, they more often found themselves here.

A situation to which Vincent didn't object. All of his previous affairs had been of the most casual sort, and he rather liked seeing some of his spare clothes hung in the wardrobe, bright against the more somber tones of Henry's suits. It made him feel as if perhaps moving from New York to Baltimore had been the right thing to do. As if he might again find the sort of home he'd once enjoyed as an apprentice, after James Dunne rescued him from the streets of the Bowery.

Assuming Henry didn't leave him behind.

Henry caught Vincent's hair in his fingers, tugging him down for an urgent kiss. Henry's mouth tasted of whiskey, his tongue hot and wet as it slid against Vincent's. Vincent shaped Henry's form, shoving beneath his coat to catch his slender hips and pull him tight. The hard ridge of Henry's erection pressed against Vincent's own, and he ground against Henry, receiving a moan for his efforts.

"I want you," Henry breathed when their lips parted again.

The words made Vincent's heart speed. "What do you want from me?" he asked, lust thickening his voice.

Henry's pale skin flushed pink, whether from the whiskey, the heat of a July night, or desire Vincent didn't know. All three, most likely. "Everything," he growled, and kissed Vincent again.

Vincent wished he could give it to Henry. The fame and recognition Henry craved. The dream they'd shared in front of the poster.

He hadn't told Henry when he applied for membership in the Psychical Society. Not because he wished to hide anything; it simply slipped Vincent's mind during the chaos of the move from New York.

Then the letter came. Oh, it was polite, as such things went, but still sent a clear message. The Baltimore Psychical Society was for whites only.

He'd kept the rejection a secret from Henry and lied when Henry suggested he join. The thought of confessing to his lover he'd been turned away because of the color of his skin etched his veins with an acidic mixture of anger and shame.

Henry wouldn't have stood it for a moment. He would have been furious, would have sworn never to speak to a single member again. Probably would have written Dr. Kelly an angry letter. All of which would spell disaster for *S, N, & D*.

Tonight's triumph meant great things for their business. New connections. New opportunities. And if the price was Vincent keeping his mouth shut, he would pay it. Grudgingly, perhaps, but it was how the world worked.

He pushed the dark thoughts aside. Tonight they celebrated, and he refused to let his lingering anger sour Henry's moment of triumph. Vincent dragged Henry to the bed, shedding clothes as they went. The breeze wafting through the light curtains was a blessing against his naked skin. He ran his hands over Henry's shoulders, avoiding by habit the still-painful scars where a bullet tore through flesh and bone last January. He ducked his head, kissing his way down Henry's throat, his cock swelling with anticipation when Henry tipped his head back to give him access. The taste of salt and sweat filled Vincent's mouth as he sucked first on one pink nipple, then the other, biting and worrying until Henry moaned softly beneath him. He made his way down farther, pausing to nibble at the ticklish spot on Henry's belly and getting a strangled curse for a reward.

He sat back for a moment to admire his handiwork. Without the shields of his gold-rimmed spectacles, Henry's eyes looked oddly vulnerable, their blue a thin ring around pupils gone wide with desire. Vincent's bites marbled his pale skin with spots of red. His nipples were hard nubs, his prick dark against his belly.

"Mmm, what a sight you are." Vincent licked his lips slowly, watching from beneath his eyelashes as Henry tracked the movement hungrily.

"I could say the same of you," Henry replied. His hand went to his cock, stroking slowly. Moisture glistened around the slit. "Just looking at you tries my control."

Vincent bent down and licked away some of the slickness from the tip of Henry's cock. "And what would you do, if you lost control?"

Henry's face reddened. Vincent lost any shame at an early age, but Henry's upbringing had been rather more refined. Still, he was beginning to come around with suitable encouragement from Vincent. "Fling you down and bugger you until you spill."

Vincent tugged at his own prick, hips thrusting forward both to tease Henry and in response to the pleasure of his hand. "Do it."

CHAPTER 2

HENRY ROLLED to his knees, catching Vincent against him for a passionate kiss. Vincent groaned into his mouth, rubbing his cock against Henry's belly. "I adore the way you kiss me," he said, when Henry gave him the space to speak again. "I've told you that, haven't I?"

"Many times," Henry replied. "But don't stop. I like hearing it." He kissed Vincent again, then ran his lips down Vincent's throat, avoiding the silver amulet Vincent had worn for the last year.

He released Vincent to rummage in the dresser for the jar of petroleum jelly. Vincent took the opportunity to stretch out on the bed, stuffing a pillow beneath his hips in order to offer an easier angle. Drawing his legs up, he hooked his hands around the backs of his knees.

Henry's eyes flashed with lust at the sight, and his hands trembled visibly as he slicked his fingers. But his touch was sure against Vincent's passage, gliding around the ring before pushing in. Vincent let out a moan of his own at the invasion. Henry knew all the ways to make him gasp and cry out, and he put them to good use.

Vincent had never had a lover who knew him so well. He bit his lip to keep from crying out too loudly when Henry entered him. The stretch felt marvelous, waves of pleasure spreading through him as Henry worked in deeper and deeper. Henry's hands gripped Vincent's hips, sweat darkening his hair. The soft glow of the night candle dusted the short hairs of Henry's arms in gold and outlined the muscles of his chest.

Vincent let go of his legs in favor of clutching Henry's forearms, tugging him closer.

"Is it good?" Henry gasped. His lips remained parted, as if begging for a kiss or a cock.

"Amazing," Vincent said, barely able to form a coherent sentence. "Feels good, Henry. Don't stop—ah!"

His words ended in a soft cry as Henry wrapped one hand around his prick, giving it a long stroke. Vincent arched his back, fingers digging into Henry's arms, awash in pleasure. It felt good, to be touched by someone who knew him this intimately, to be filled by someone he cared for, and he hoped cared for him. Henry's hips rocked more urgently, driving in harder, and his fingers tightened on Vincent's cock. It was too much, and Vincent bit back a shout as the wave of ecstasy crested, hot semen spilling out and over his belly. Henry gasped his name, pushing in and stilling, their bodies locked together in a single circle of heat and desire.

The sound of their ragged breathing filled the little room. Henry sat back, dipped a finger in the spend pooled on Vincent's stomach, and brought it to his mouth. Vincent grinned at him lazily, feeling boneless and content. He wanted nothing more than to close his eyes and drift off into blissful sleep.

But he couldn't. Vincent rolled to his feet with a groan, and went to the bag of salt sitting on a shelf near the door.

He'd spent most of his life sleeping without lines of salt across the doorway and window sills. But ever since the night last year, when Dunne died and the ghost that killed him vanished, Vincent never slept without a barrier of salt. He couldn't shake the fear the ghost still lurked out there, waiting to complete the job it began.

Maybe it was foolish. Henry didn't seem to think so, indeed went out of his way to provide salt for the nights Vincent stayed over. But did he really believe something stalked Vincent, or did he consider it a delusion on Vincent's part? Certainly there was no evidence the ghost even lingered in this world, let alone had any interest in Vincent.

But the memory of Dunne's staring eyes, face purple from the ghost squeezing the life out of him, sent a slick surge of fear down Vincent's spine. The spirit had used his hands to kill Dunne. What if he awoke some morning and found Henry lying beside him, eyes glazed and throat bearing the marks of his fingers?

Vincent bent over and hurriedly began to pour the line of salt in front of the closed door. Even if Henry only humored him, at least he didn't point out that Vincent Night was afraid of the dark.

Henry rose with the dawn. Vincent, who seldom moved from bed before noon, rolled over to Henry's vacated side, mumbled incoherently, and fell back asleep with his face buried in Henry's pillow.

Henry shaved and dressed quietly, then paused by the bed before letting himself out. The white linens gleamed next to Vincent's sienna skin, the sheets thrown back to reveal shapely limbs and long muscles. The sight of him stole Henry's breath and softened something in his chest, and he leaned down and tenderly swept a lock of hair back from Vincent's face. Vincent sighed softly but didn't wake.

Henry suppressed a sigh of his own. He should have confessed the truth about his failure before they made love. Instead, he'd let himself be carried away by passion, unable to think of anything beyond pleasure.

Well, no. There was pleasure, but not just of the physical sort. He... *enjoyed* didn't seem a strong enough word, but it would do. He enjoyed Vincent's company. Making him smile and laugh, and groan in ecstasy. And drifting off in his arms, and waking up the same way.

He needed to confess. To see Vincent's disappointment, and hope...what? That Vincent didn't regret throwing his lot in with Henry? Didn't break off their relationship and carry on with Maillard instead?

Assuming he wasn't already, depending on what sort of "performance" Maillard referred to last night. Ministers wrote long letters to the newspaper, ranting against the debauchery accompanying séances. Although hardly the orgies painted by the over-active imaginations of self-appointed moral guardians, the accusations did hold a kernel of truth. A small group of adults, sitting in a dark room, tension high as they waited for a ghost to appear, created a definite atmosphere. The holding of hands, the long black cloths draped over the séance tables, heightened the possibility of illicit activity. Spirits drew on sexual energy—as Henry knew first hand, given what Vincent did to him during a séance at Reyhome Castle.

They'd made no promises to one another, outside of their business contract. Perhaps Vincent already grew bored with Henry. Vincent went to art salons and drank coffee with poets. He already knew half the musicians in the city, white and colored, and felt at home in the company of his fellow aesthetes like Christopher Maillard.

Whereas Henry attended scientific lectures, read every new journal article on electromagnetism, and preferred to be at home and in bed by nine o'clock. Could he really be surprised if Vincent took advantage of the opportunities afforded him?

Henry suppressed a groan and let himself out. A sitting room separated the two bedrooms, and many mornings he found Jo sitting there, studying scientific journals. Her late mother had gifted Jo with a genius for mathematics, along with tightly curled hair and chestnut skin. This morning, however, the chamber lay empty.

The downstairs floor was divided into two parts: the occult shop out front, and Henry's workshop in the back. A second building in the yard just behind the shop offered an alternate place for him to work, when the chemical smells or sounds might otherwise disrupt séances or disturb any customers.

He found Jo in the back room, working on an idea of her own: a headlamp such as miners used, but with a small arc light in place of a candle. A yellow scarf kept her hair out of the way, and matched the cheerful hue of her dress. The apron covering the front of the dress was, as usual, stained from grease and chemicals, with small holes eaten in the fabric by acid.

To Henry's surprise, as she usually shared Vincent's sleeping habits, Lizzie was there as well. She wore a long, flowing dress, corseted tightly about the waist to lend her figure a certain shape nature had not provided. A wide choker matched the dress, and golden hair hung in soft ringlets about her face and shoulders.

"Of course you can borrow my earrings," she said to Jo.

"Earrings?" Henry asked. "What on earth do you want earrings for, Jo? Don't you already have a pair?"

Jo and Lizzie exchanged a look. "See?" Jo asked.

"You didn't have to convince me," Lizzie replied. "Your cousin has no sense of fashion whatsoever. I'd hoped Vincent might prove a good influence, but I fear it isn't to be."

Henry tugged self-consciously at his coat tails. His clothing might not be exactly new, but nothing was frayed, and there were surely more important things for him to spend his money on, anyway. The memory of Maillard's stylish cream suit flashed through his mind, but he put it aside sternly.

"My wardrobe is fine, thank you," he said. "Should I go for coffee and pastries?"

"Without even telling us how things went at the Psychical Society?" Lizzie asked, raising a brow.

Jo all but bounced on her stool. "Yes, tell us all about it, Henry!"

His tongue lay thick in his mouth. "I…"

"It was a triumph, of course," Vincent said from the stairs behind him.

Startled, Henry turned. Vincent stood there, clad in his silk oriental robe, his hair still mussed from sleep. A proud smile curved his lips.

Of all the days for Vincent to actually rise before noon.

"I knew it!" Jo leapt up and hugged Henry, her thin arms surprisingly strong around his waist.

"Well done," Lizzie agreed. "I will admit, I was a bit skeptical when Vincent pled the case for us to go into business with you."

"After my behavior at Reyhome Castle, you had every right to be," Henry said faintly.

"Indeed," she agreed. "But it seems Vincent was right about you."

Oh God. He wanted to sink through the floor, or burst into flames, or perhaps just fall down stone dead.

"And Vincent, really, put some clothes on," Lizzie went on, oblivious to Henry's distress. "Wandering about in nightshirt and robe in front of two ladies! Your manners are deplorable."

"It's not scandalous," Jo protested. "Vincent is family. Right, Vincent?"

Vincent tugged affectionately at Jo's scarf. "Right, Jo."

Henry's heart plummeted even further. The disaster at the Psychical Society last night wouldn't just affect him, would it?

After Jo's parents died in a railway accident, she'd first gone to their aunt. The wretched woman behaved as if President Lincoln never freed a single slave, and considered Jo her property rather than her niece. When Henry dared write to the girl, Aunt Emma tried to warn Jo off by telling her the family rumors of his proclivities. Jo decided Henry the lesser of two evils, and showed up on his doorstep shortly thereafter. The matter of Henry's preferences had never come up...until Vincent.

Far from being repulsed by him, Jo adored Vincent. If he left, it wouldn't only be Henry who ended up with a broken heart. And while Henry and Lizzie might not precisely be friends, she and Jo had formed something of a bond.

"Put on some trousers, Vincent," Lizzie ordered. "Jo and I will go to the café and fetch breakfast."

Vincent waited until Lizzie and Jo left, before giving Henry a kiss. "Good morning," he murmured against Henry's lips. "You don't seem to be feeling the effects of last night too badly."

"No." Not the way Vincent meant, anyway. "Are you?"

"A bit of a headache." Vincent pressed against him more tightly. "A little bit of an ache somewhere else."

Heat flooded Henry's face. "I'm sorry—"

"I'm not. I like it when you get enthusiastic." Vincent nipped Henry's lower lip gently with his teeth.

Henry pushed him away. "You'd better go and get dressed, before Lizzie and Jo return."

"I suppose." Vincent's hand skated lightly over the growing bulge in Henry's trousers. "You could join me."

"Dear heavens, no!" Henry exclaimed, mortified. "I mean—we don't have time before the others get back—they'd know—"

Vincent laughed. "I rather imagine they know already," he said with a wink. "But have it your way."

Henry turned to the workbench, determined not to admire the sway of Vincent's backside as he made his way up the stairs. As the familiar silence of the shop settled around him, he slumped onto the stool Jo had vacated. Parts lay in front of him, a scatter of batteries and acid flasks, the carbon electrodes for Jo's headlamp, and spools of copper wire.

He began to sort through the jumble, as though imposing order on the workbench might do the same for his thoughts. Parts to one side, completed tools to the other. The ghost grounder lay buried beneath a pile of loose wire, its copper rod slightly tarnished from disuse.

How dare Dr. Kelly accuse him of *reducing* the "beloved dead," as Kelly put it, to mere electromagnetic impulses? The ghost grounder worked by draining the electromagnetic energy of spirits—wasn't that proof enough that they were comprised of electrical impulses, no different from the activity of the human brain in life?

Scowling at the tarnish, Henry put aside the grounder and began to sort the loose copper wire by gage. He just wanted to save people the heartache he'd gone through as a lad—was that so wrong? Why shouldn't they protect their families from unscrupulous fake mediums by detecting themselves whether a cold spot came from a spirit or a badly fitted window? Or sleep peacefully, knowing Strauss's Sure-Fire Spirit Finder would warn them of ghostly activity?

But it all cost money. His gaze went to the dispeller, with its crystalline wafers and electrodes and batteries, and God, why did everything have to be so damned expensive? Purchasing the shop had eaten through the five hundred dollar prize from Reyhome Castle, and a good deal of their personal savings as well. Business since had been just enough to buy parts and keep food on the table, but no more. Last night had been supposed to fix all of that, give them the money to manufacture his devices and keep the shop afloat.

The copper wire bent in his hands as he tightened his grip on it. He'd failed, then *lied* about it, and now everyone thought prosperity was right around the corner. What had he been thinking? He had to confess, but how on earth was he to do so?

There came a knock on the front door, despite the closed sign. Grateful for the distraction, Henry set aside the wire and went to answer it. Heavy drapes covered the windows, blotting out the sunlight that would interfere with a séance and preventing him from seeing who stood on the stoop.

"We're closed," he said automatically as he opened the door.

The man outside possessed a plain face, remarkable only for a luxuriant mustache and mutton chops. His suit and top hat were of excellent quality, if a bit drab in color. A carriage waited on the street behind him.

Henry straightened automatically. Whoever this fellow was, he obviously had money to spend.

"Forgive the intrusion," the man said, extending his hand. "But I come to you on a matter most urgent. Allow me to introduce myself. John Emberey, at your service."

"Henry Strauss," Henry said automatically. Up close, the lines of strain framing Emberey's eyes became visible. "What might I do for you?"

"Your partners." Emberey glanced at the sign above the door. "Vincent Night and Elizabeth Devereaux, correct?"

"Yes."

"Oh, good." Some of the tension left Emberey's shoulders. "Another medium referred Mr. Night and Miss Devereaux to me. We— the company I work for, that is—are having a problem with a ghost."

Politeness dictated Henry invite Emberey inside. Possibly even up to the sitting room, given the quality of his clothing.

The sitting room beside Henry's bedroom, where Vincent even now dressed for the day. There was no possible means of explaining such a thing.

Each back alley encounter with another man had been tainted with the fear of being caught, or of the other fellow proving to be a police officer tasked with luring and then arresting men on an indecency charge. Henry hadn't realized just how pleasant the last few months truly had been, until faced once again with the fear of discovery.

"Er, I'm afraid my partners haven't arrived just yet," Henry lied, trying not to fidget. "Rather than force you to await them, perhaps it would be more convenient for us to come to you?"

If Emberey was disappointed, he didn't show it. "How very kind of you to offer. I've taken a room at the Altamont Hotel. I must impress upon you the urgency of the case. A man may already be dead."

"May?" What did Emberey mean?

"I'll explain everything at the hotel."

Did Emberey exaggerate, or was the situation truly dire? "Of course," Henry said. "I'll summon them right away. We'll join you within two hour's time, you have my word."

As Emberey's carriage clattered away, Henry shut the door slowly. There came the soft whisper of shoes against the thick rugs covering the shop floor. Vincent stood in the doorway, fastening his cufflinks. "Well. I wonder what the devil that was about?"

CHAPTER 3

THE PORTER who escorted them onto the hotel veranda gave Vincent a disapproving look, which he ignored. He was well used to receiving such stares, from men who couldn't quite decide whether to judge his skin or his fashionable clothes. Generally they chose the clothes, more worried about angering someone who might have influence than about keeping out an Indian.

Emberey awaited them at one of the tables. Despite the early hour, the day had already grown warm, and a pitcher of lemonade sweated on the table beside him. The humid breeze stirred the feathers on ladies' hats, and touched the skin on the back of Vincent's neck with welcome coolness.

"Mr. Emberey," Henry said. Emberey's clothing was uninspired, but that was to be expected from a man of business. On the other hand, it was clearly of the highest quality, which suggested there might be profit to be had. "This is Mr. Vincent Night."

Emberey's expression didn't change—apparently whoever had recommended them had mentioned Vincent's race. Emberey's palm felt soft against Vincent's. Whatever work he did, it wasn't with his hands.

"And Miss Elizabeth Devereaux," Henry went on.

Emberey bent gallantly over her hand. "Miss Devereaux, a pleasure. Thank you for coming."

They took their seats, and Lizzie folded her hands in her lap. She sat very straight, her face shaded by a Leghorn hat, the shadow softening her features. "Mr. Strauss said you asked for us by name, sir?" Her tone was slightly stiff.

"Oh, yes, of course." Emberey flushed lightly. "Please, forgive my presumption. Miss Devereaux, Mr. Night, you were recommended to me by another medium. Mr. Sylvester Ortensi."

Vincent shifted to the edge of his chair. "Sylvester?"

"I share in your loss," Sylvester had written on the card of condolence he sent on learning of Dunne's death.

And, years earlier, *"You've chosen well, James. Both of your apprentices have immense talent."*

Sylvester had never been a constant in their lives, not like Dunne. More like a genial uncle, who appeared on occasion with treats and jokes, only to vanish a few days later.

"I see," Lizzie said.

Henry frowned in confusion. "I don't recognize the name."

Emberey peered closely at Henry. "The Great Ortensi? Master of the Spirit World? A medium who has performed before the crowned heads of Europe?" he said in disbelief. "Surely in your line of work you must have heard of him."

Henry flushed. "I-I've devoted my time more to the scientific aspects," he stammered.

Vincent took pity on Henry. "He was a close friend of Dunne's. We've known him for quite some time." Vincent turned to Emberey. "And you say he recommended us to you?"

"In a way." The man cleared his throat. "Allow me to start at the beginning. I represent Mr. Robert Carlisle, who is in the process of building a steel mill in Devil's Walk, Pennsylvania." Emberey laughed weakly. "Perhaps I should have taken the name as a sign. Mr. Carlisle hired me to oversee construction—to be his eyes and ears in Devil's Walk. The area is quite rural and remote at the moment, but has abundant quantities of coal. A nearby railroad line and a waterfall to generate electricity made it the perfect site. Upon my arrival, I heard rumors that the ghost of a woman from colonial times haunted the woods. Naturally I paid no attention."

Vincent accepted a glass of lemonade from the porter. "Naturally."

Emberey gave him a sharp look. "Let me be frank. I'm not a superstitious man. I believe most tales of the supernatural are mere fancies. An odd breeze, the scream of a barn owl, a branch knocking against a window—these are the sources of the vast majority of ghost stories."

"Quite right," Henry said quickly. "I'm sure my colleagues will agree that genuine hauntings are far more rare than folklore would have us believe."

Vincent barely restrained himself from rolling his eyes. "I take it this case proved to be different."

"The men began to complain almost immediately." Emberey scowled, as if personally insulted by the fears of his workers. "They claimed tools went missing, only to be found in strange places later—in the high branches of trees, or sealed inside crates, that sort of thing. Every accident, from the shifting ground that caused a wall to collapse, to a carpenter taking off a finger with his saw, was put down to the work of the ghost." Emberey snorted. "Of course I put no stock in it. Indeed, I became quite angry at the foolish superstition interfering with progress."

Would the man never get to the point? "But something happened to change your mind," Vincent prompted.

"I fear so." Emberey glanced around, as if worried at the prospect of being overheard. "I wouldn't believe it if I hadn't seen it from my window, but the apparition of a burning woman appeared in the very main square of the town. I realized there were indeed otherworldly forces at work."

Henry's lips pursed. "I don't wish to disagree," he began.

"I very much doubt it," Vincent murmured.

Henry shot him another annoyed look. "People posing as spirits have used phosphorescent paint in order to glow in the dark, which might explain your 'burning' woman."

Emberey frowned. He didn't strike Vincent as the sort of man who liked being contradicted. "Had you been in my place, I assure you, you would be a believer as well, sir," he said, rather coldly. "Naturally the townspeople were hysterical. I was forced to threaten to call in strike breakers in order to get them back to work the next day. This sort of disruption is terrible for business, so I wrote to Mr. Carlisle. It was he who hired Mr. Ortensi. As soon as he arrived, Mr. Ortensi assured me there is indeed a ghost."

Henry angled his head toward Vincent. "And you two vouch for him?"

"He's no fraud," Vincent replied. "Sylvester—Mr. Ortensi—is a genuine medium."

"If you already have Mr. Ortensi assisting you, why come to us?" Lizzie asked. "What's happened?"

"There was a close call with a séance," Emberey said. "The spirit burned Mr. Ortensi's hands, though only mildly. And now one of the workers is missing. If it were a simple laborer I'd assume him lying drunk in a ditch somewhere, but Mr. Norris is a skilled surveyor. He went into the wood to look over the sites where the worker housing will be constructed. He hasn't returned in two days."

"Couldn't he have simply quit? Become frightened by his own imaginings and run away?" Henry asked.

Emberey shook his head. "He's a local man, though I hired him in Pittsburgh. His parents still live in Devil's Walk, and he stays with them. They've heard nothing from him. Naturally, they're frantic, and search parties have beat the woods for him since yesterday morning, when it became clear he wouldn't return on his own. Progress on the mill has virtually come to a standstill. Mr. Ortensi and I agreed something must be done, and he gave me your names. I came here, while he remained behind in case the ghost tried anything further. Will you come?"

Lizzie hesitated. "Our shop—"

"Mr. Carlisle is prepared to pay quite handsomely for your time," Emberey said. "Every day work fails to progress costs the company a considerable sum." He withdrew a sealed envelope from his jacket and passed it to Vincent. "Inside is a letter from Mr. Ortensi. He asked me to give it to you, whether or not my plea moved you to give an immediate answer."

Vincent took the envelope, its fine stationery heavy against his fingers. Wax sealed the flap. The symbol of the all-seeing eye Sylvester had adopted long ago stared up at him.

"Very well," Lizzie said, rising. The men hurried to their feet as well. "We will confer together, and give you our answer by this afternoon. Good day, Mr. Emberey."

Vincent stared down at the letter in his hand, but he didn't see the words. Just a small room, utterly different from the back of the shop where he currently sat. In the room of his memory, a fire crackled to drive back the cold of the New York winter. He pushed open the door, then froze. An unfamiliar man sat across from Dunne.

Dunne glanced up and a welcoming smile appeared on his face. "Ah, there you are, my boy," he said. "Come in. There's someone I'd like you to meet."

Vincent's hands trembled, so he tucked them behind him before they gave away his fear. Dunne hadn't laid a hand on him the entire four months Vincent lived in the house. But in his experience, two men waiting in a room for him was never a good thing. Maybe Dunne just liked to watch.

"This is Sylvester Ortensi," Dunne said, gesturing to the other man. "He's a medium, like us."

At least Ortensi was handsome enough, his brown hair clean and his hazel eyes unclouded from drink. Maybe this wouldn't be too bad.

"I'm pleased to meet you, Mr. Ortensi," Vincent said, pronouncing the words carefully.

"The world will judge you on two things," Dunne liked to say. *"Your appearance and your speech. The sad truth of the world is that your skin means you'll have to work at both much harder than a white man. The right clothes and the right accents will make the path easier."*

"And I, you, Vincent." The smile Ortensi gave him was kind, and not at all lascivious. Vincent allowed himself to relax fractionally. Maybe Dunne didn't mean to hand him over to his friend after all. "James tells me you're exceptionally gifted. And a very hard worker."

An unfamiliar pleasure went through Vincent. "Thank you, sir," he mumbled.

"Chin up, Vincent," Dunne said, although his tone remained gentle. Vincent obeyed, and put his shoulders back a bit, too. A smile from his mentor was his reward.

"Where is Edward hiding?" Ortensi asked Dunne.

Vincent's belly clenched, but Dunne only said, "She prefers to go by Elizabeth now. And she's hiding because her hair hasn't grown out yet, and she's convinced she looks wretched."

Ortensi laughed. "Ah, the young. I should go and regale…Elizabeth, you said?…of my time in Siberia, collecting legends from the mediums there. Among the Yakut, spirit workers are expected to live in a manner opposite of the sex they were born."

"Anything you can say to help will be welcome," Dunne said fervently. "It hasn't been an easy time for her. Not that society will ever make it easy, but, well. I fear for her."

"Then I shall speak to her at once."

Ortensi left. Dunne beckoned Vincent closer. "Sylvester is an old friend of mine," he said. "We apprenticed together."

"Like me and Lizzie?" Vincent asked. "I mean—sorry—like Lizzie and me?"

"Exactly," Dunne replied, with another of those rewarding smiles. "Should anything happen to me while you're still in my care, Sylvester will see to your welfare. You can trust him."

"Vincent?" Lizzie asked softly.

Vincent blinked back to the here and now. Henry, Jo, and Lizzie all stared at him. Henry and Jo seemed puzzled, but Lizzie wore a sympathetic expression on her face.

"Old memories," Vincent said.

Henry's lips parted in concern. "Bad ones?"

"Actually, no. Quite the opposite." He cleared his throat and turned his attention to the crisp stationery he'd drawn from within the envelope. Like the seal, the letterhead bore an all-seeing eye and "The Great Ortensi" in huge letters.

Sylvester understood showmanship, just as Dunne had. The difference was Sylvester parlayed it into fame and fortune, while Dunne chose a quieter life, away from the limelight.

My dearest Vincent and Elizabeth, he read aloud.

I hope this letter finds you both well. It grieves me not to have been free to visit you before you left New York. Word of your move surprised me, I'll admit, but perhaps there is more to Baltimore than I'm aware of.

"Hmph," Henry muttered, folding his arms across his chest. "Baltimore is hardly some backwater."

Vincent hid a smile. "I'm sure he meant nothing by it. Shall I continue?"

"Please," Lizzie said, shooting a quelling look at Henry.

I'm sure Mr. Emberey has already told you of the situation in Devil's Walk. I'd heard the legend before, of course—

Vincent broke off. "Sylvester collects folklore about hauntings and the like," he explained to Henry and Jo. "And not just here in America—he's traveled the world, talking to anyone who would answer his questions."

"If there's a story Sylvester hasn't heard, it isn't worth hearing," Lizzie agreed.

"Devil's Walk is in Pennsylvania." Henry turned to Jo. "Have you heard of it, Jo?"

Jo's brow furrowed beneath her scarf. "I think I might have," she said slowly. "We visited Pittsburgh once or twice, when Daddy had business there, and I saw it on a map. But I don't really know a lot about the western side of the state. And I didn't hear any legends." She shrugged. "Sorry, Henry."

"No need to be. It was only a thought."

Vincent cleared his throat. "If I may continue?"

—but never had the opportunity to explore the area and verify its truth. I can now say with confidence there is a haunting, as attested to by the bandages on my fingers.

The spirit is powerful and the sad truth is I'm not as young as I once was. I would be very grateful to have your assistance in this matter. The owner of the land and mill, Mr. Carlisle, is no happier over the situation than Mr. Emberey, and wishes it taken care of as quickly as possible. As for myself, I fear innocents may be injured, should this ghost not be dismissed soon. My sense is this haunting could very easily turn dangerous—even fatal. Assuming it hasn't already.

I would be deeply in your debt if the two of you would consent to travel to Devil's Walk and aid me in this undertaking. And if it isn't possible, please at least send a letter back via Mr. Emberey, so I might know you're thriving in your new surroundings. Even though you're grown, I can't break the habit of worrying for you both as if you were children.

Yours most truly,

Sylvester

Lizzie's green eyes met Vincent's, and he read in them the same thoughts that echoed through his skull. Sylvester and Dunne apprenticed together, under the same master. That bond meant something. Sylvester cared about them. He'd brought back presents from all over the world, stayed up late telling them tales from far off lands, and faithfully mailed postcards when he couldn't visit.

The visits and postcards waned over the last few years, which seemed only natural. Vincent and Lizzie were no longer apprentices, but full mediums, their childhoods left behind. Sylvester, who never took an apprentice of his own, had a busy life, filled with appearances before the crowned heads of Europe. But some bonds couldn't be broken with the mere passage of time.

"I'll send word to Mr. Emberey," Lizzie said. "Vincent, check the train schedules."

"It seems the decision has been made," Henry said.

"All else aside, Sylvester needs our help," Vincent replied with a shrug. "I'm sure you and Jo will do fine running the shop while we're gone. Obviously you can't conduct séances, but at least you'll be able to sell books and incense."

Henry paled sharply, his eyes widening as if Vincent had slapped him. "Don't be absurd. Jo and I will accompany you."

Vincent's heart leapt—foolishly, perhaps. Lizzie only frowned. "Someone should remain and run the shop," she replied. "Vincent and I have an obligation. You don't."

This time Henry's eyes narrowed behind their shields of glass. "This 'Great Ortensi,' or however he styles himself, says the situation is perilous. Do you truly think I'd let you, *either* of you, walk into danger while I remained behind in safety?"

Vincent grinned. "That's my Henry. Clever *and* brave."

Henry flushed scarlet. Behind his back, Jo pantomimed having a swooning fit. Vincent barely resisted the urge to stick his tongue out at her.

"I don't know about that," Henry mumbled. He took off his glasses and cleaned them with his handkerchief, as if the gesture would distract from his blush. "And…if you think…I mean, if you fear my inventions will hinder rather than help…"

"Why on earth should we think such a thing?" Lizzie demanded. "Dear heavens, you're practically the next president of the Psychical Society, after last night. If the three of us are agreed the shop can survive being closed for a week or more, by all means, join us."

It would be tight, money-wise. But it seemed this ghost had Mr. Carlisle by the short hairs, and as his representative, Mr. Emberey as well. Sylvester called the pay generous, so it would likely be more than they could earn remaining here.

"Thank you, Henry," Vincent said. A curious thrill ran through him at the thought of introducing Henry to Sylvester. Like bringing home a betrothed to meet the family.

Which was absurd. He had no claim on Henry, and certainly not of that sort. Pushing the foolish thought out of his mind, he sat back and met Lizzie's eyes. "It's decided. The four of us will go together to meet whatever awaits us in Devil's Walk."

CHAPTER 4

VINCENT REMOVED his coats and shirts from Henry's wardrobe, carefully folding them in his trunk. He'd finish packing at his apartment tonight; in the morning, they'd catch the train to Devil's Walk with Emberey.

And he'd see Sylvester again. For the first time since Dunne's death.

"Vincent?" Henry asked quietly from the doorway.

Vincent turned. Henry's face wore an uncertain look, his brow furrowed beneath the lock of honey colored hair, which tumbled free across his forehead. "Is everything all right?"

"Of course it is." Vincent gave him a quick smile. "Unless you count the fact I won't be able to take all my clothes with me. Tragic."

Henry rolled his eyes and came further into the room. "Truly how you will suffer." His expression softened. "You just seem...melancholy."

A flippant answer came to Vincent's tongue. He would have voiced it to anyone else without second thought and hidden the truth down deep, where no one else could see. But he'd never been able to hold Henry at arm's length the way he had his other lovers. "I'm worried."

"About your friend? This Great Ortensi?"

"He was always just Sylvester to us. And yes." Vincent realized he was in danger of crushing the velvet of the coat in his hands and quickly relaxed his grip. "I haven't seen him since...since Dunne died."

"They were close?"

"They apprenticed together." But that explanation wouldn't mean anything to Henry. How to put it? "Sometimes mediumistic talent runs in families. But more often, the medium has to seek outside training. It can be rather...intense, for all involved."

"I understand." The floor creaked as Henry crossed to him. "Dunne was like a father to you."

"A father I killed," Vincent said, placing the coat carefully in the trunk.

Henry put a hand to Vincent's arm. "Stop blaming yourself. It wasn't your fault."

Vincent didn't bother to argue. Lizzie had told him the same thing, again and again. A malevolent spirit possessed him. He had no control over his body when his hands wrapped around Dunne's throat and squeezed.

Having a strong mediumistic talent paradoxically made him both more powerful and more vulnerable at the same time. He could summon ghosts at a séance with barely a thought, channel them, and send them back to the other side. It was simply easier for them to slip in and out of his skin.

Even if they didn't mean him—or anyone else living—any good.

Dunne tried to banish the spirit, but he'd been too slow. They'd expected an ordinary poltergeist, not whatever hellish thing had met them.

Dunne paid the price, and Vincent wore a silver medallion to keep the ghosts out, every moment of every day except when conducting a séance. But he had started to channel again, and he'd made peace with losing the shop in New York, the last thing of Dunne's they'd owned.

And now Sylvester came back into their lives.

"I owed Dunne a debt," Vincent said, picking carefully through the words as if the wrong one might cut him. "He saved me from a life that would have been 'nasty, brutish, and short' as the saying goes. The truth is, I'll never know what he saw in me, to make him offer to become my mentor."

Henry's arms slid around his waist from behind. "He saw a boy with a good heart."

"I wish." Vincent put his hand on Henry's. "You don't know what I was like then. And I'm damned thankful for it." Henry's chest pressed against Vincent's back as he drew breath to argue. "I know you're going to contradict me, but you're missing the point. I owe Dunne everything. With him dead, whether or not you think me responsible, the debt transfers to Sylvester."

"That doesn't make sense," Henry said. "Mr. Ortensi isn't the one who scooped you up off the streets."

Vincent sighed. "I know it doesn't make sense to you. I'm not even saying the debt is the same. But the closest I can come in this life to repaying Dunne is to help Sylvester."

Henry remained silent for an uncharacteristically long time. Then he shifted, resting his cheek against Vincent's back. "I see."

Did he? Perhaps he did. Henry understood family and debts—why else would he have taken in Jo? The rest of the family had turned their backs on Henry for doing so—or, more accurately, for acknowledging her as his cousin and not presenting her as an unrelated maid or housekeeper. Of course Henry obviously loved Jo now. But he'd given her a home before he'd known anything more about her than she was his cousin and in need of a safe harbor.

His willingness to help, his compassion, was one of the things that drew Vincent to him from the start. Well, that and the way his backside filled out his trousers.

"I'll do what I can to help you and put an end to this haunting," Henry said after a long moment. He tightened his arms around Vincent, before letting go.

"Vincent!" Jo shouted from below. "The cart driver wants to know how much longer you'll be!"

Vincent grabbed the handle of his trunk. "I'd best go, before he leaves without me and I have to lug the trunk all the way to my apartment."

Henry took the other end. "Let me help you down the stairs."

At the bottom of the stair, they paused. Henry leaned in and gave him a quick kiss. "I'll see you tomorrow at the train station."

A part of Vincent longed to say he'd return after packing, to spend the night. But to come back here, just to return again to his apartment in the morning to collect his things, would be ridiculous. Still, once the trunk was secure in the back of the cart and the driver started off, Vincent couldn't help but look back over his shoulder for one last glimpse of Henry. But his lover had already gone back inside the shop, so Vincent turned back to the fore, feeling strangely alone.

Henry stared out the train window as night fell over the countryside rushing past. Jo slumped dozing against his shoulder. Her head rocked with every jolt of the car, and he couldn't imagine how she could sleep through such jostling.

They'd changed trains at the new Baltimore and Ohio Station in Pittsburgh. The bustle of the city gave way to farms dotted across low hills. Soon the hills grew steeper, the slopes covered by dark forests, and even the occasional lights of distant farmhouses vanished.

Vincent sat across from him, beside Lizzie. He stretched his foot out to nudge Henry's ankle. "Are you all right, Henry?"

Henry turned from the dark landscape to the warm light of the car. "I'm fine."

Vincent met his gaze, thick, black brows drawing down. "You've been rather quiet."

Henry dropped his eyes, unable to meet Vincent's searching look. He glanced at Jo, intending to use her rest as an excuse…but as she'd slept through the steam whistle and Emberey droning on about the steel mill, he doubted Vincent would believe him. "Travel tires me," he lied. "A good night's sleep will restore my mood."

He turned again to the window, so Vincent wouldn't see the sick, crawling feeling that had lingered in his stomach ever since the night of his presentation. He'd dedicated his life to making certain no one would ever be taken in by a spiritualist fraud again, thanks to the application of science.

And yet now he'd become a fraud himself. Vincent, Lizzie, everyone believed him the darling of the Psychical Society. They'd brought him here under false pretenses, thinking he'd been vindicated rather than cast out.

And he'd let them believe it.

But what else could he do? If he'd chosen to reveal his deception, surely they wouldn't have brought him with them to Devil's Walk. And from Ortensi's letter, it sounded as though the ghost had already inflicted some sort of injury. Not to mention Emberey's suggestion it might have killed, or at least harmed, the missing surveyor. If something went wrong, if Vincent were hurt and Henry not there to help…he couldn't bear the thought.

The train began to slow, and within a few minutes rattled to a halt. The view out the window looked less than promising, the depot nothing more than a tiny platform exposed to the elements. A few lights burned beyond, but for the most part there was only the night-shrouded countryside.

Henry nudged Jo. "Time to wake up, sleepyhead."

She rubbed her eyes and sat upright. "Umph. Are we there?"

"Yes. And you drooled on my shoulder."

"I did not!" She swatted him on the arm.

"Welcome to Devil's Walk, ladies and gentlemen," Emberey said, rising to his feet from where he sat beside Lizzie.

"It's very...rustic," Vincent said as they stepped onto the platform.

"That's one word for it," Lizzie muttered.

Henry eyed the muddy track, where a coach awaited them. Beyond lay a cluster of buildings, which appeared to be a mix of houses and shops. "I expect it will grow once the steel mill is built," he said.

Emberey overheard. "We've already made some improvements to the town. Some of the locals had reservations about the steel mill, including one or two influential families. We needed to demonstrate the progress we'd bring. Devil's Walk now has not only a clock tower, but a moon tower atop it."

Vincent regarded the dark town. "I would have expected it to put out a bit more light," he drawled.

Emberey scowled, perhaps thinking him impertinent. "The house I rent fronts the square where the tower is, and the cursed thing kept me up half the night. When something went wrong with the arc lamp, I ordered it left alone. We'd already begun construction on the mill, so why waste the coal keeping the thing running when it had accomplished its purpose?"

"Oh," Jo said, obviously disappointed.

Henry turned away to watch the porters unload their baggage. He hadn't known precisely what to bring, and thus packed as many of his devices as seemed practical. Anything might turn out to be useful. Perhaps something of his might even prove decisive in removing the ghost. If it did, might it mitigate Vincent's anger when he finally learned of Henry's deception? Might this venture offer Henry the chance to redeem himself?

"Hurry it, boys!" one of the porters shouted to his fellows. "The sun's down—the ghost could be anywhere!"

"Please, be careful!" Henry exclaimed as they began shoving crates hastily onto the platform. "Some of my equipment is quite delicate!"

"Any breakage will come out of your pay," Emberey shouted with a glare at the porters. The men gave him a few dark looks, and there was some grumbling, but they handled the rest of the baggage much more carefully.

When the last bags were loaded, they climbed into the coach and started through the town. Most of the buildings appeared to be postcolonial in construction, but whatever prosperity led to the town's founding, it had passed the area by long ago. Other than the train depot and the clock tower, Henry didn't see any buildings less than fifty years old.

The clock chimed as they rattled past. The brick tower itself was of respectable height, topped by metal scaffolding forming a second tower to support the darkened arc lamp.

"That's quite an erection," Vincent remarked blandly.

"We're very proud of it," Emberey agreed.

"I imagine you are," Vincent said. Henry bit his lip to keep from snickering.

Jo leaned past Henry to peer out the window. "I wish we could have seen the moon tower in operation," she remarked wistfully.

Lizzie picked at a loose thread on her gloves. "Surely they have arc lights in Philadelphia."

"Yes, but nothing quite so tall. They're meant to light smaller spaces, not an entire town."

The streets were deserted, save for a last pedestrian who all but ran to his door and slammed it behind him. Despite the heat, shutters covered most of the windows, as if to keep out whatever might prowl the night.

"These people are frightened," Lizzie observed.

"Very," Vincent agreed. He adjusted his tie, but Henry recognized the gesture as a surreptitious way of checking that the silver amulet still hung about his neck.

If Henry meant to impress his partners, he should try to put a good face on things. "Lucky we came," he said with as much confidence as he could muster.

Vincent's mouth curved, as if he suppressed a laugh.

"It had better be," Emberey said. "Mr. Carlisle is paying a great deal of money to have you here. Hopefully you'll be more effectual than the Great Ortensi has been thus far."

Vincent's smile slipped away into a frown. Lizzie's hands tightened slightly where they rested in her skirts, but her hat hid her expression.

The carriage rattled to a halt in front of the hotel, which appeared to be the newest structure visible since the clock tower. The door swung open, and a carpet of golden light poured out. Henry climbed from the carriage, followed by Vincent and Emberey. Vincent paused to help the ladies, and porters swarmed from the hotel to take their baggage. Hoping to keep out of the way of the bustle, Henry stepped away from the crowd.

Someone seized his shoulders, wrenching him backward. A moment later, his spine collided with the hotel's clapboard siding. Rough hands pinned him in place. Breath laden with alcohol blew into his face.

Henry froze, heart pounding madly. Was he about to be robbed? The corner of the hotel blocked the carriage lights. He could make out only the edge of an unshaven jaw, an uncombed rat's nest of hair, and the gleam of angry eyes.

"You," the man growled into his face. "Are you one of the mediums?"

"N-No," Henry gasped truthfully. "But I came with them—"

"Then I'll give you a warning." The man shook him, hard enough Henry's teeth clacked together. "If you value your life, go back where you came from. There's evil here, and the witch is coming for those men who've lost their souls to the devil already. If you try and protect them, there'll be no mercy on you."

"I—I—" Henry stammered.

"Get away from him!" Vincent shouted.

Henry's assailant let out a startled grunt and released Henry. Teeth bared and nostrils flared, Vincent hauled the man back. The ruffian tried to shove Vincent away, but Vincent refused to let go, clutching the man's coat with one hand.

The other he swung straight into his opponent's face.

The man let out a cry of either fury or pain. He struck at Vincent, but Vincent moved too fast, weaving out of the way like a snake.

"Enough!" Emberey roared. Striding past Vincent, he grabbed the stranger and shoved him back. "Crawl back into the bottle, Fitzwilliam, or I'll have the sheriff down to deal with you."

"This is God's judgment!" Fitzwilliam wiped at his split lip, and his cuff came away stained in blood. "You're all murderers!"

Fury hardened Emberey's features. "I've given you far too much license, out of pity for your loss. But this will cease immediately, or you'll spend the next month staring at the bars of a jail cell."

Fitzwilliam spat at Emberey's feet. Taking a step back, he met Henry's gaze. "Remember what I said," he growled. "This is the Lord's judgment. Leave Devil's Walk if you don't want His wrath to fall on you as well."

"Are you all right, Henry?" Vincent couldn't resist taking a step toward his lover, although he managed to restrain his desire to touch

Henry's face. "Did that brute hurt you?"

He'd helped Lizzie and Jo from the coach, turned to say something to Henry, and realized Henry had vanished. For a moment, he'd thought Henry already inside the hotel. Then he'd caught a glimpse of a man standing just around the corner. He'd stepped closer and seen a stranger, pinning Henry to the wall, and…

And the next few moments were a blur of white-hot rage, until Emberey stepped in.

Henry adjusted his spectacles. "I'm fine," he said, although his voice shook slightly. "Thanks to you." A small smile touched his mouth, and his eyes warmed. "That was…impressive."

"It's been a while since I've had the occasion to use my fists," Vincent admitted. His knuckles stung. He flexed his fingers to make certain they all still worked.

"Henry!" Jo ran up and grabbed Henry's arm.

"I'm fine, Jo," he said, patting her shoulder. "But what on earth was —Fitzwilliam, I think you said, Mr. Emberey?—on about?"

Emberey's eyes narrowed as he watched the shadows where Fitzwilliam vanished. "An agitator who believes we should halt the march of progress," he said disgustedly.

"I'm not sure what you mean," Henry said as they started back to the hotel entrance.

"Constructing a steel mill is a difficult undertaking, Mr. Strauss." Emberey paused to knock the mud from his shoes, before stepping inside. "In such an endeavor, accidents are inevitable. Part of a wall collapsed, and three men lost their lives. Mr. Fitzwilliam's son was one of them."

"How awful," Lizzie murmured as they stepped inside.

"Don't waste your sympathy," Emberey said. "If he isn't in a drunken stupor, he's shouting the witch is bringing God's judgment down on our heads."

"Quite the theological knot," Vincent said. "But what is this about a witch?"

"The ghost is supposed to be some sort of witch woman." Emberey waved an impatient hand. "Peterson! Is Mr. Ortensi here?"

"He's waiting in the private parlor, sir," said a man Vincent took to be the hotelkeeper.

"Good, good. Take my guests to him." Emberey inclined his head to them. "As for me, I must return to work. I'm certain a great many things needing my attention have piled up in my absence. Mr. Ortensi knows how to contact me, should you need anything further."

He departed. Peterson inclined his head to them. "The porters have taken your things to your rooms," he said. "If you'll follow me."

A slight air of shabbiness clung to the hotel interior, the curtains faded from sunlight and the carpets a bit threadbare, but an improvement over most of the apartments Vincent had rented. Certainly it was much better than the overcrowded tenements he'd lived in as a child in the Bowery.

Peterson led the way past a small saloon, currently deserted. The fear that had descended over Devil's Walk seemed to be keeping even the most dedicated drinkers home. Beyond lay the private parlor. A fireplace, currently cold, dominated one wall. A great pair of antlers hung above the mantel. Taxidermy owls and wild cats stared down from the walls with glass eyes. A table had been laid for dining. At its head sat Sylvester.

CHAPTER 5

THE YEARS had added gray to Sylvester's temples, lines about his eyes, and a slight paunch to his figure. But the same smile still greeted them, the same voice exclaimed, "Vincent! Elizabeth!"

He held open his arms. Vincent embraced him, closing his eyes tight against the unexpected burn of tears. "It's g-good to see you," he said.

Sylvester hugged him. He smelled of hair tonic and something spicy, probably cologne from some exotic port. "I'm so sorry about James," he whispered, and for a moment Vincent thought his resolve would crack, and he'd embarrass himself by crying on Sylvester's shoulder.

"Thank you," Vincent managed. He pulled away to let Lizzie have her turn, surreptitiously wiping at his eyes.

"Sylvester," he said, when Lizzie finished her greeting. "Let me introduce Miss Jocelyn Strauss."

Sylvester took Jo's hand and bowed over it extravagantly. "My sojourn in Devil's Walk has been worth it, to meet such a rose."

Jo's cheeks darkened, and she giggled.

Vincent grinned. "And this is Jo's cousin and our partner, Mr. Henry Strauss."

Sylvester smiled and held out his hand. Bandages swathed his hands, although he seemed to have the use of his fingers. Still, Henry took it gently. "A pleasure to meet you," Henry said.

"And you," Sylvester replied. A little frown creased his forehead. "I must admit, I was surprised when Mr. Emberey's wire said you would be joining us."

"You must have gotten my letter after we moved to Baltimore," Lizzie said, taking a seat at the table beside Jo.

"I did, and I recall your explanation of Mr. Strauss's little inventions," Sylvester said. "I'm merely uncertain what use they'll be of here."

Henry's nostrils flared, and Vincent winced. Before Henry gave vent to his offense, Vincent said, "I assure you, Sylvester, Mr. Strauss has *many* talents."

Henry flushed red. Lizzie rolled her eyes. "Henry's machines have proved quite useful," she said. "Trust me when I say Vincent and I were rather skeptical at first as well. But Henry has convinced us, not to mention the finest minds in the Baltimore Psychical Society."

Rather than looking proud, Henry turned even redder. Vincent would have expected him to shout his accomplishment from the rooftops. Instead, he'd been strangely reserved about the matter.

But why? Surely the Psychical Society hadn't mentioned their rejection of Vincent. Henry would have quit the society on the spot.

Wouldn't he?

Vincent sat beside Sylvester, with Lizzie across from him. A waiter appeared and offered the hotel's menu, a choice between beef and lamb. Sylvester approved a bottle of wine, and the waiter began to pour.

"Lemonade for Jo, if you please," Henry said.

Jo gave him a pleading look. "But Henry…"

"Wine isn't suitable for young ladies," he said primly. "You may have lemonade or tea."

Sylvester chuckled. "Having become used to continental ways, it is sometimes odd to return to American temperance," he told Jo sympathetically. "Still, I'm sure your cousin only wishes the best for you. How did you find the journey here?"

They settled into a round of small talk, while the waiters bustled in and out, bringing them drinks and, in short order, dinner. When the last of the staff retreated, shutting the door after him, Henry turned to Sylvester.

"Mr. Emberey said your injury came from attempting a séance?" he asked.

"I fear so," Sylvester replied as he cut into his lamb. "Did Vincent or Lizzie tell you of my talent?"

"They only said you apprenticed with their mentor," Henry replied.

"Sylvester is clairsentient," Vincent explained. "He receives impressions from ghosts, both emotional and physical. Usually the latter manifest in his hands."

Sylvester smiled ruefully. "Quite. Although ordinarily they're but sensations. In this case…well. There's a reason I sent for help."

"What did it do to you?" Lizzie asked.

"It burned my hands." Sylvester's smile was gone now, his face grave. "For the spirit that walks here is a creature of fire, both within and without."

Ortensi held up his wine glass. "The tale begins with the fire of passion," he said. His deep voice was mesmerizing, and Henry understood how he must hold the attention of his audiences. A gold ring showed from beneath one of the light strips of gauze, and the gaslight caught on the ornate pocket watch pinned to his vest. His exquisitely tailored clothing contrasted rather sharply with Henry's shabby suit. Even Vincent's carefully measured fashion couldn't compete. Clearly all of those performances in front of the crowned heads of Europe paid well.

"Devil's Walk wasn't the original name of this place, nor this the original town," Ortensi went on. "Over a hundred years ago, a colonial village stood not far from here, at the base of the waterfall Mr. Carlisle wishes to utilize for his steel mill. Whispering Falls, it was called, the site of a small but prosperous enough town. There was a mill at the falls, and a church, and fertile fields surrounded by forest."

"Even more horribly bucolic than now," Vincent remarked, holding out his glass for more wine. He'd barely touched his lamb. "How ghastly."

Ortensi chuckled. "Quite. At any rate, as the story goes, two women named Mary and Rosanna fell in love with the same man. Zadock, the mayor's son and the handsomest bachelor in the village, gave his heart to Rosanna. Alas, Rosanna had only her heart to give in return. She was the daughter of a charcoal burner whose death left her with nothing save a tiny hut within the surrounding forest. Mary, on the other hand, was the miller's daughter, her family second only to the mayor's in money and prestige."

"Allow me to guess—he married the rich one," Lizzie said dryly.

"You guess correctly." Ortensi paused while the waiters returned to lay out their dessert of apple pie. "Rosanna was heartbroken—and vindictive. She swore she would have her revenge on the man who had wronged her. The incidents began soon after the wedding. Zadock and his young wife heard the sound of someone—or *something*—beating against the outside of their house. But when he went to investigate, he found no trace of either animal or man. The sounds continued, night after night, as if something sought entrance."

Ortensi paused. "Until the night they began to come from inside the house."

Jo shivered. Henry patted her hand. "Don't let it frighten you."

"I'm not frightened," she said quickly. He suspected the statement wasn't entirely true, but let it go for the moment.

"The situation grew steadily worse," Ortensi went on. "Bed clothes were violently ripped back, pillows tossed about. An invisible entity began to slap and pinch Mary, leaving terrible bruises all over her body."

Now it was Vincent's turn to shudder. "It sounds like a poltergeist," Lizzie said.

"On the surface of it," Ortensi agreed. "As vicious as the attacks against Mary were, Zadock bore the worst of them. He was thrown about and struck, waked constantly from sleep, hounded day and night by unseen forces. And not just within his home. When he and Mary fled to her parents' house, their invisible attacker followed them."

Alarm flashed over Vincent's handsome features. "It doesn't sound like a poltergeist."

"No, it does not. Nor does what happened next. Mary awoke one morning to find her husband dead at her side. Strangled by otherworldly hands."

All the blood seemed to drain from Vincent's face, and he sagged against his chair. "God," he murmured.

The similarities to the spirit that had used Vincent to kill Dunne were painfully clear. Henry wanted to put an arm around Vincent for comfort. But of course he couldn't, so he said, "Are we sure? Perhaps Mary did away with her husband herself, and blamed his death on unseen forces."

"I repeat only the words of the legend, Mr. Strauss," Ortensi replied, a bit coolly. "I have no way of proving or disproving them at this late date."

"Of course. Please continue." But he glanced at Vincent, who stared blindly at his uneaten apple pie. If only they were alone.

"Times were different then," Ortensi went on. "Less than a century before, men and women accused of witchcraft hung from the gallows at Salem. The people of Whispering Falls knew of the suffering of Mary and Zadock, and had long turned a dark eye toward Rosanna. They called her witch, and wondered if her hand lay behind the couple's torment."

"But surely that's absurd," Henry said. "How could Rosanna be responsible for the actions of a spirit? Even if she were a medium, the best she could do is summon one from the otherworld, not cause it to go on a murderous rampage."

Ortensi looked less than pleased at the interruption. Lizzie had half-lifted her glass, but now set it down again. "Necromancy," she said

Vincent shivered.

"I'm familiar with the term, of course," Henry said. "But are you saying it's…well, real?"

"There are always rumors." Ortensi steepled his bandaged fingers before him. "Legends. Tales of talismans that allow the living to command the dead. Even someone with no mediumistic talent can use them to control spirits on this side of the veil, although supposedly the spirit in question must have some connection of blood or bone to the talisman. Needless to say, in the hands of a medium they can do a great deal more."

"So Rosanna had one of these talismans?" Jo asked.

"Perhaps. *If* she was responsible at all, and not an innocent victim, blamed for things beyond her control." He paused to sip his wine again. "If I may continue?"

Clearly the man wasn't used to anyone interrupting with questions. "Please," Henry said.

"Zadock's death was the final straw," Ortensi said. "The old laws against witchcraft had fallen before the onslaught of reason, but reason and legality meant little to a group of terrified and angry villagers. They dragged Rosanna from her house. Foregoing the noose, they chose the Inquisition's method of disposing of a witch."

"Fire." Lizzie's face took on a greenish cast, and Henry suddenly wished he hadn't eaten quite so much pie.

Ortensi nodded gravely. "She burned, and they celebrated to the sound of her screams. When night fell, they went to their homes, congratulating each other on ridding the world of a dangerous evil. They didn't think to make certain the fire went out. The autumn had been a dry one, and the fallen leaves provided plenty of tinder. In the deepest part of the night, flames roared through Whispering Falls. Half the town was engulfed before anyone knew it. Beds became pyres."

Ortensi stared down at his bandaged hands. "Only a few townspeople survived, all of them children. According to the legend, when they were found days later, hungry and terrified, they claimed unseen hands shoved their parents back into the burning houses, while allowing the children to escape."

Henry frowned. "Is that…possible? Even a very angry spirit surely shouldn't have so much power."

Ortensi let out an exasperated sigh. "As I said, Mr. Strauss, I but repeat the legend. Most likely it has grown much in the telling. But ever since, it's said the devil walks in these woods. The original village was utterly abandoned, and the surrounding forest consumed the remains. The townsfolk I spoke with claim any hunters venturing within would sense unseen eyes upon them. They whisper of being chased by a dark shape, or of becoming separated from companions who stepped only a few feet away."

"And now the haunting has spread into the town," Lizzie said thoughtfully. "But none of the original incidents occurred on this land?"

"No. Why she's chosen to leave her forest and walk the streets of the town, I couldn't say. When I tried to contact her…" Ortensi displayed his wrapped fingers. "I sensed her anger. The heat of her pyre against my skin. Before I knew it, the heat turned to pain. I broke the circle, but not before she'd managed to harm me. The burns are mild, but if I'd waited for even a few seconds longer, I fear the damage would be far worse."

Henry studied the bandages. "And such power to harm you through your gift is unusual? Forgive me, but I don't know much about mediumistic talents."

"And yet you work with two mediums," Ortensi said.

Henry flushed at the delicate note of censure in the older man's voice. "I leave such matters to Vincent and Lizzie," he said.

"Of course," Ortensi replied mildly. Did he mean to imply Henry should have taken the time to study such things, or did Henry read too many of his own fears into the man's tone? "Physical injury occurs only when the spirit the clairsentient is sensing is both very powerful and very malevolent. I've had it happen only twice before, and both times in my youth, when I practiced far less caution than I do now. You see why I chose to send for Vincent and Elizabeth. And you, of course."

"Of course," Henry replied stiffly. It seemed obvious enough from his earlier remarks that the Great Ortensi saw no more use for Henry's "little inventions" than Dr. Kelly and the Psychical Society.

But he would show Ortensi wrong. Show them all wrong. He would prove himself, and Vincent would forgive his foolish lie, and everything would be fine. "Do you have any ideas as to how to deal with the ghost?"

"A few." Ortensi shifted in his chair. "But I'm certain you're all very tired. We'll confer over breakfast as to our best course of action."

"Mr. Emberey seemed to think the matter urgent," Henry countered.

"It's late, and I'm exhausted," Lizzie replied. "Not to mention, when dealing with a powerful spirit such as this, we're far better off waiting until daylight. She'll be weaker then."

Outvoted, Henry could only nod. As they rose from the table, Ortensi said, "Vincent? Elizabeth? If you'd care to catch up...?"

"I will bid you good night," Lizzie replied, with a fond smile for Ortensi. "We'll have plenty of time later."

"Of course. Vincent? A drink in the saloon, perhaps?"

"I'd love to," Vincent said.

Henry paused by the door, waiting for an invitation from Vincent to join them. It wasn't forthcoming, and Ortensi didn't even glance at him when they passed by.

Did Ortensi really want to talk to Vincent and Lizzie about old times, or had he some other purpose behind excluding Henry? Did he intend the mediums should make their plans tonight, without Henry present?

"Henry, are you coming?" Jo called.

Henry took a deep breath. He was being paranoid, surely. Ortensi had no reason to exclude him from anything.

And if he tried, he'd find Henry not so easily dissuaded.

"To James Dunne," Sylvester said, when the barkeep set the whiskeys in front of them.

Vincent clinked glasses with Sylvester, then downed the shot. Maybe its warmth would chase the cold from his belly.

"I can't believe it's almost been a year," Vincent said, motioning for the barkeep to refill his glass. A year of wearing the silver amulet, save for when he channeled during a séance. A year of salting his doors and windows every night before bed.

A year of feeling as though the thick, oily substance of the dark spirit that possessed him still stained the inside of his skin. Of fearing the taste of rot and slime, of blood and wet bone, would bloom again on his tongue.

"James was a good man," Sylvester agreed. "The world is lesser without him in it."

"The best," Vincent agreed. "He saw something worthwhile in

everyone he ever met." Even Vincent.

"Yes." Sylvester tugged at the bandage on one finger, revealing the bright pink of scalded skin. "We could use more men like him. We had such plans...it grieves me he won't be here to see them come to fruition."

"Plans?" Vincent leaned forward curiously. "He never mentioned any such things to us."

"I think he wanted to wait until everything was in place, before mentioning it to you and Lizzie." Sylvester swirled the whiskey in his glass. "Let's just say some of my trips to more obscure corners of the world held a purpose beyond simple curiosity."

"Oh." Vincent sat back, unsure how to feel about this revelation. He'd believed Dunne shared everything with them. This sounded important, like something Dunne and Sylvester had worked on together for years.

And yet Dunne never mentioned it to Vincent, even once.

"As soon as we're done here in Devil's Walk, I'll explain everything fully, to you and Lizzie both," Sylvester went on. "I hope you'll agree to help me. I could certainly use your assistance, now that James is gone."

"Of course," Vincent said immediately.

Sylvester smiled. "Don't you want to hear what you're agreeing to first?"

"I don't need to. If it was something Dunne thought important, that's enough."

"I'm glad to hear it, my boy." Sylvester took a sip from his whiskey. "And I'm glad to have you here. Although your friend Henry..."

Vincent took another sip of whiskey. Henry had been in rather a mood over dinner, although Vincent wasn't entirely sure why. Perhaps his distrust of mediums colored his perceptions of Sylvester.

"Henry can be a bit of a challenge," Vincent said wryly. "But I assure you, he has only the best of intentions. His methods are unconventional, but there is merit to them."

"I see." Sylvester turned his tumbler in a circle, as if studying the light reflecting in the depths of the whiskey. "If you say he is trustworthy, of course I'll accept your judgment."

"I'd trust him with my life. Have, in fact." He hesitated, but it needed to be said. "Henry doesn't have as much practical experience as the rest of us when it comes to actually dealing with the spirit world, however."

Sylvester's look sharpened. "How much?"

"Our work at Reyhome Castle and a few séances after," Vincent admitted.

Sylvester's mouth tightened. "Vincent, this is a dangerous affair. It's no place for an amateur."

"Henry is learning," Vincent insisted. "And he's no fool. He has a level head and keeps his wits about him when things go badly. I saw it for myself at Reyhome."

"I'm sure you did." Sylvester sighed. "Truthfully, though, I hoped to speak with you and Elizabeth, not only to catch up, but in order to plan for tomorrow."

Vincent frowned. "I don't understand. Henry is our business partner. We want him included."

"I know. I only wish you'd spoken to me before your move to Baltimore." Sylvester tilted his glass, watching the golden liquid within shift. "The truth is, I'm no longer young. My face has become a familiar sight on tour posters, and the public always wants something new. It's hard to compete with fresh-faced young ladies, even if they have little talent as either true mediums or as fakes."

The weariness in his voice drew a sympathetic wince from Vincent. "I'm sorry, Sylvester. I didn't know."

"I thought about asking you to join me, after James died. The three of us together might offer something new...but Lizzie has good reason to stay out of the limelight I thrive in, and I knew you'd never leave her. Or the shop."

Vincent shook his head. "I wouldn't have been any use to you. I stopped channeling for a while. As for the shop...we lost it anyway, but you're right. I wasn't ready to let go of it yet."

"Still, if you'd only come to me after Reyhome..."

Would Vincent have said yes, if Sylvester approached him then? The tender words he and Henry had spoken to one another at Reyhome seemed tenuous in Henry's absence. And after weeks of silence, Vincent had concluded their brief affair at Reyhome had merely been a bit of passing fun.

Then Henry showed up on his doorstep, and Vincent's heart took wing just at the sight of him.

"You'll understand more when you see Henry's instruments in action," Vincent replied. "He's a brilliant man, truly."

"An unusual one, at least. I was surprised to hear his cousin introduced as such." Sylvester hesitated. "*Is* she his cousin?"

"Of course!" Vincent scowled, and Sylvester held up his hands quickly. "And just as brilliant in her own way. Henry's white family have ostracized him for acknowledging the relationship, but he said Jo needed him more than he needed them."

"You seem very fond of him," Sylvester observed.

Vincent glanced down at his whiskey. "Dunne would have loved him."

"I'm sure he would have." Sylvester drained the last of his whiskey and put down the glass. "But enough. If you have such faith in Mr. Strauss, I will give him a chance as well."

CHAPTER 6

RATHER THAN retire to his bed, Henry opened one of the crates the porters had stacked in his room. Ortensi might dismiss Henry's devices out of hand, but it would be harder to do so if the medium actually saw one of them in operation.

He removed a set of Franklin bells and the glass dome meant to protect them from wind, thankfully still intact after the long train ride. Carrying them in his arms, he sought out the hotelkeeper.

Peterson stood near the front door, talking quietly with the clerk and one of the porters. "…the damned ghost," Henry heard, before the clerk nodded in his direction. The hotelkeeper turned to him with a hasty smile.

"Is everything in order, sir?" he asked, peering at the set of bells in Henry's arms.

"Quite," Henry replied. "But I thought I might be able to offer you —and any guests—reassurances the ghost hasn't approached the hotel. Or at least, a warning if she does."

"Can you do that, sir?" the porter wondered.

"This device will ring if the ghost is nearby. Or a thunderstorm," he added honestly. The Franklin bells reacted to changes in the electromagnetic field. Unfortunately, he had yet to find a way to get them to differentiate between changes caused by ghosts and those caused by lightning. "I'll need to place it outside, attached to one of your lightning rods."

"Please, sir," the night clerk said to Peterson. "It'd put my mind at ease, having to stand here all night, wondering if the ghost is coming back."

"Of course," Peterson said. "Come, Mr. Strauss. I'll show you where the nearest lightning rod is."

Installing the Franklin bells was but the work of a few moments. After making certain the glass dome was secure, Henry went back inside, to the profuse thanks of the night clerk.

Vincent's voice drifted out as he passed the saloon. No telling how long he'd be up, reminiscing with Ortensi. Returning to his room, Henry changed into his nightshirt and threw the coverlets back.

He ought to lie down and try to sleep. Not sit up and wait for the sound of Vincent's door, conveniently located next to his. There was no reason for him to feel on edge. Vincent was just having a drink with an old friend.

An old friend with an expensive suit, fancy pocket watch, and a history of performing before the crowned heads of Europe.

"Do you think that will be us, someday?"

Ortensi had it all today.

Henry took a deep breath and calmed his racing heart. He'd gotten himself into this mess. He'd get himself out of it, by proving his worth to Vincent and Lizzie.

And Jo. When she found out Henry had lied…

His imagination supplied a look of betrayal, which soured his heart. God, anything but that.

Footsteps sounded in the hall outside, and a moment later, there came the soft click of the key in the lock of the neighboring room. Henry rose hastily and eased open his own door. Vincent paused, the gaslight at the end of the hall gilding his dark hair. There was no sign of Ortensi; perhaps his room lay on a different floor.

Henry gave him a questioning look he hoped conveyed his meaning. A slow smile crossed Vincent's full mouth, and he nodded.

Henry slipped from his room and into Vincent's, just as Vincent pulled the curtains tight across the window, to prevent anyone from glimpsing them together. The rooms were tiny, no more than a narrow bed, washstand, and clothespress. While Henry threw the bolt, Vincent removed his coat, shook it out, and hung it up carefully. *Clothes make the man,* he once told Henry. Especially if the man had skin of a darker shade. A shabbily dressed Indian would be sneered at, or—for all Henry knew—might even face being dragged off to a reservation somewhere. Impeccable fashion formed the key Vincent used to open doors that would otherwise be closed to him.

Henry sat on the edge of the bed and watched while Vincent undressed. Cuffs, collar, vest, bracers, shirt, and trousers all followed the coat. His ochre skin glowed in the soft light of the night candle, contrasting with his cotton drawers. The sight made Henry's chest tighten and his breath hitch, and not just from lust.

For years, his only contact with men who shared his inclinations came in the form of a hasty tug in some back alley, both of them going their own way as quickly as possible after. No kisses or kind words. No caresses. No watching while the other man undressed for bed, his movements calculated to tease.

"You didn't eat much at dinner," he said.

Vincent shrugged. "I wasn't hungry."

"I thought seeing Mr. Ortensi again might have brought back memories of your mentor." Dark memories of the man's death.

Surprise flickered across Vincent's face, before vanishing behind a smile. "You don't need to worry about me."

"Of course I do," Henry said simply. "I care about you."

Vincent's lips parted, eyes widening slightly, as though the words caught him off-guard. Surely he understood Henry's regard for him? Then Vincent's expression melted into a warm smile. "Thank you for the concern. But we have much more interesting things to talk about tonight. For example, you could tell me if you like what you're seeing?"

Henry swallowed against the tightness in his throat. "I do like. Very much."

Vincent shed his drawers; his cock stood half at attention. "Surely you don't mean to deprive me of the same pleasure?"

Henry hurriedly slipped off his nightshirt. Vincent sat on the bed by him, pulling him in for a kiss. Vincent tasted of whiskey and cinnamon, his lips soft against Henry's. Desire fired through his blood, washing away the lingering bitterness of jealousy. Whatever the future might hold, tonight Vincent was his. And he would take full advantage of the fact.

Vincent pulled back, his breathing rough and uneven. "Who's in the next room?" he whispered. "Do you know?"

Henry nodded. "Lizzie, thank heavens. We'll still have to be discreet, but..."

"But not worry too much about the occasional moan or creak of the bed," Vincent agreed with a sly grin. "And I mean to make you moan,

Mr. Strauss."

"Do you, Mr. Night?" Henry challenged, although in truth he had no doubt Vincent would do exactly that.

Vincent cupped the back of his head, dragging him in for a rough kiss, before shoving him back onto the bed. Henry tumbled onto the surprisingly soft mattress, and Vincent wasted no time straddling him.

Just the sight of him made Henry's mouth water. How he'd attracted the attention of someone like Vincent Night, he still didn't know. Vincent's body was lithe and muscled like a dancer's, all lean, hard muscle clinging close to the bone. His long hair framed the strong bones of his face, and thick lashes accented the dark heat of his eyes. The sheen of sweat from the warm room made Vincent's skin look dusted in gold.

"You're beautiful," Henry said as Vincent bent over him. The silver amulet hung between them, spinning slowly in the light.

Vincent's hands splayed over Henry's chest, shaping the fan of his ribs, pausing to tweak one nipple, then the other. Henry whimpered, hips jerking in response, but Vincent's weight kept him pinned to the bed. "So are you," Vincent said.

Henry's cheeks warmed. He was all too aware of his own lack of any particular charms. Still, something about him had caught Vincent's eye during those hectic days in Reyhome Castle. What, he couldn't imagine.

Vincent's grin widened. "How I love to see you blush." He traced Henry's lower lip with his thumb. "The way you bite your lip when you're busy thinking."

He did? Henry hadn't even been aware of it. He sucked Vincent's thumb into his mouth and was rewarded with a low growl of desire.

Vincent pulled his thumb away and kissed Henry, hard. Henry moaned into his mouth, then sucked on Vincent's tongue when it slid past his lips. Vincent's hips jerked in response, and a rush of pleasure and pride went through Henry, to make this man want him so.

Vincent pulled away, bracing his hands on Henry's shoulders. Their cocks rubbed together, slickness from their slits trailing along Henry's stomach. "Wrap your hand around us," Vincent urged, and Henry obeyed.

Vincent began to move against him, a slow slide of hips. The friction of their pricks against one another wrung a soft gasp from Henry. He drowned in sensation, Vincent's length rutting against his. Henry caught slickness from the tip of Vincent's cock, using his thumb to smear it over the head. Vincent gasped and picked up the pace. The bed creaked beneath them, faster and faster. Vincent looked utterly wild, his hair disheveled, his eyes hot with lust.

"Vincent," Henry whispered, although in truth he wanted to scream it at the top of his lungs.

Vincent seemed to understand; his kiss-swollen lips twisted into a feral grin. "Yes, Henry," he crooned. "You're going to come for me, aren't you? Come for me!"

Henry's lips parted, and he barely bit back a cry as his balls tightened. Pleasure shot through him, hard and fast as a lightning strike. Vincent thrust against him, until the sensation became too acute. Henry shifted his grip, letting his softening prick fall against his stomach, forming a tunnel for Vincent's length with his spend-slicked hands.

Vincent's jaw clenched, and his eyes squeezed shut. A shudder went through him, and with a low groan, he shot into Henry's grip.

The tension left his arms, and he half-collapsed against Henry. "Mmm," he mumbled, and turned his head for a tender kiss.

"Good?" Henry asked against his lips, once the kiss ended.

"The best." Vincent snuck another kiss. "Stay a little while? I know you have to leave before morning, but surely…?"

The longing in his voice tightened a band around Henry's throat. "Of course. Here—let's put down the salt, before we drift off. I set up Franklin bells outside the hotel, by the way, against the wall. We should get a warning if anything approaches, but I'll still wake you when I get up. You can lay the salt down again behind me."

A sad little smile touched Vincent's mouth. "Thank you, Henry. You take such good care of me."

He wanted to. God, more than anything. He wanted to be the man Vincent thought him. The one to make all of Vincent's dreams come true.

"Don't be silly," he admonished weakly. "Now come—the sooner we get the salt in place, the sooner we can sleep."

Vincent woke from a deep sleep, the sound of the Franklin bells ringing madly in his ears.

He jerked upright, hand going to the amulet about his neck before he even fully awoke. The silver burned cold in his hand, and the air of the room went from summer to winter. The night candle guttered sullenly, its flame sickly blue.

The taste of ashes and overdone pork flooded his mouth, courtesy of his clairgustance, and he barely kept from gagging.

Henry stirred beside him. "Vincent? Do I hear the bells?"

"Yes," Vincent whispered. His breath turned to steam. "The ghost is close. I can sense her presence."

Henry went still. "Where? She can't have gotten past the lines of salt on the windows."

It had been foolish to fall asleep together and risk being caught, but at the moment Vincent could only feel grateful for Henry's solid presence. He slid out of bed and snatched up his nightshirt, before tossing Henry's to him. The boards felt like ice against his feet, and the taste of ash and burned flesh turned his stomach.

"Where is it?" Henry repeated. "How close does a ghost have to be for you to sense it?"

It was such a Henry question to ask, Vincent would have laughed if not for the searing cold. "I can't say I've ever measured it."

Was the spirit inside the hotel? Curse it, he should have warned the hotelkeeper to put down lines of salt at all the doors and windows. The ghost hadn't entered any buildings yet, as far as he knew, but the precaution should still have been made.

Henry pulled on his nightshirt and spectacles. Vincent motioned for Henry to remain still, and turned all his attention to listening. Only the ordinary creak of settling beams came from inside the hotel. No screams or startled cries sounded. Just the wild ringing of the Franklin bells outside.

There came a low scrape, like a fingernail against glass.

Henry started beside him, and Vincent grabbed his hand automatically. The sound came again, its pitch grating on Vincent's nerves.

"The window," Henry whispered, his breath puffing in the icy air. He stared fixedly at the tightly drawn curtains. One bare foot slid across the floor, edging closer to the aperture.

Nothing. Just the bells, ringing their frantic alarm.

Henry glanced at Vincent, then back to the window. His hand trembled visibly as he reached out and brushed the fabric back just an inch.

A white eye, without iris or pupil, stared in at them.

Henry sprang back with a startled oath. The curtain tangled in his fingers, wrenching it aside and revealing the horror in full. A woman pressed against the glass, her red hair streaming flames. The skin of her face bubbled from heat, and her eyes were nothing but pallid, cooked orbs that still conveyed a terrible malevolence.

"Oh God!" Henry staggered back. Vincent caught him, pulling him close.

"She can't cross the salt line on the window sill," Vincent said, grateful his voice remained steady.

Henry nodded. "Y-Yes. Of course."

The ghost opened her mouth. Her lips split wider and wider, gaping far larger than a human mouth should.

She *screamed*.

The sound pierced Vincent's ears like knitting needles. He dropped to his knees, dragging Henry down with him, as the glass in the window exploded. They grappled for a wild moment, each trying to shield the other from the flying shards. The stench of burning pork filled the room, accompanied by a blast of hot air contrasting painfully with the icy cold of a moment before.

Silence. Even the bells had stilled.

Vincent's forehead pressed against Henry's, and he stared into his lover's blue eyes for a long moment. The taste of ashes faded slowly from his mouth.

"She's gone," he said, and this time his voice did shake.

Shouts of alarm came from the rooms around them, and more distant ones from the night staff. "Go," Vincent ordered, and shoved Henry toward the door.

For once, Henry didn't argue. He flung open Vincent's door and ducked outside. A moment later, there came the sound of his door opening. "Is everyone all right?" he called. "Jo? Lizzie?"

Vincent pulled on his oriental robe and tied it about his waist as he stepped into the corridor. *"I'm* fine, thanks so much for asking," he drawled, as if they hadn't clung together just moments ago.

But it was a necessary pretense. A night porter appeared almost immediately. Although barely old enough to be called a man, and paler than the linens, the porter said, "Is everyone all right?"

"What happened?" Jo asked as she came into the hall. "That scream…"

"I heard the bells. I take it our ghost has paid us a visit," Lizzie said from her doorway. She was bundled in a thick dressing gown, and her hair spread loose over her shoulders.

"Indeed." Vincent turned to the porter. "I'm afraid I'll require another room. The ghost shattered the window in mine."

"Oh! Dear heavens, sir, are you hurt?" the porter asked, paling even further.

"I'm fine. I—Henry, where are you going?"

Henry dashed past him, wrapped in his dressing gown and holding a night candle in one hand and the satchel with his instruments in the other. "To take measurements, of course!" he shouted over his shoulder. "We must move quickly, before any phenomena have time to fade. Come along, Jo!"

"Of course, what was I thinking?" Vincent muttered. He and Jo hastened after Henry, down the hall and out into the street.

Lights showed through the cracks in a few shutters, but if the scream had awakened the townsfolk, they remained barricaded in their houses. Vincent stepped in what he hoped was mud, and cursed Henry for rushing out without sparing enough time even to dress.

Of course, he was the fool who had followed Henry out here, instead of staying inside while waiting for the porter to find him a new bed.

Henry already had his satchel open and his instruments out. "Oh, good, Jo," he said distractedly. "Take these readings." While she read the thermometer and barometer in the flickering light of the candle, Henry pulled out his portable galvanometer. "The ghost first chilled the air—gathering energy to her, no doubt—then heated it like a blast furnace. Is that ordinary behavior, Vincent?"

"I've never encountered such," he confessed. "But every haunting is different."

Henry sniffed—no doubt he thought the ghosts should fall into line and behave in a uniform fashion, which would make them easier to study.

Vincent stepped up behind him and peered over his shoulder at the instrument in Henry's hands. "What does this mean?" he asked.

"Well," Henry said uncertainly, "I haven't had time to develop enough of a baseline to say what constitutes a variation from the norm."

"You probably say that to all the ghosts."

Henry flushed and shot him an irritable look. "I don't know what it means. Yet."

Lantern light appeared at the door to the hotel. Sylvester walked toward them, accompanied by the night clerk. "Vincent?" Sylvester called. "Mr. Strauss? Miss Strauss—are you quite well?"

"Thank you, Mr. Ortensi," Jo said, not looking away from the thermometer as she recorded the slow rise in temperature. "I'm fine."

"Brave girl," Sylvester said. He'd taken the time to fling on trousers, shirt, and coat, at least. And shoes. "I take it the infernal racket that woke me was your doing, Mr. Strauss?"

"It was, sir," the night clerk said eagerly. "And grateful I am! I'd just been thinking about stepping outside for a breath of air, there not being much in the way of it at my desk. If not for the bells warning me to stay inside..." He shuddered dramatically.

"Well done then, Mr. Strauss," Sylvester said, although with far less enthusiasm than the clerk showed. "But what in the world are you doing out here now?"

"Applying science to the problem, Mr. Ortensi," Henry said, glaring at the galvanometer, as if it had done him a personal injustice by not providing the answers he sought.

Sylvester gave Vincent a puzzled look. "To what end? The ghost is gone."

"If nothing else, to gather data on the spirit world," Henry replied stiffly. "And, between Vincent sensing the ghost and the evidence of disruptions of temperature and pressure, we have established the haunting is genuine."

"We already knew as much," Vincent said, unsuccessfully trying to tamp down on his annoyance.

Sylvester stiffened at the implied insult in Henry's words. "I see, Mr. Strauss," he said icily. "And in all your haste to narrow your gaze to the small numbers of your instruments, have you bothered yet to look up?"

Vincent frowned. "What do you...oh."

Sylvester raised his lantern high, and the light spilled across the side of the hotel. Burned into the clapboard siding in crude letters were the words: BRING HIM BACK.

CHAPTER 7

"**BRING HIM** back," Lizzie mused over breakfast the next morning. "What could it mean?"

Henry stared down at his eggs and toast. Exhaustion dragged at his bones—he'd barely slept at all since the incident with the ghost the night before. Every time he shut his eyes, he imagined those awful fingers scraping at the window, those eyes like hard-boiled eggs.

His gorge rose, and he pushed the eggs aside. Toast it was.

"Who is 'he?'" Henry asked, to distract himself from the memory. "And where is 'back?'"

"It seems obvious, doesn't it?" Ortensi asked. He certainly didn't seem to be suffering from a lack of appetite, digging into a mound of pancakes with gusto. "'He' refers to Zadock, the man stolen from Rosanna by her rival. It seems over a hundred years later, she's still angry about being spurned, and her rage won't let her rest."

Lizzie stirred sugar into her coffee. An artful application of powder hid any darkness around her eyes, but the corners of her mouth drooped. "I'd be rather more angry about being burned alive, myself."

"Ghosts don't think rationally," Vincent said. Although he lounged casually in his chair, dark circles showed beneath his eyes. He'd taken only a few bites from the toast in front of him. "Those unable to cross over often become focused on a single idea or obsession."

"I'm aware of that," Lizzie said irritably. "I'm only saying she has greater cause for anger than lovesickness over some stupid man."

The toast stuck to Henry's throat, and he wished he'd put more butter on. Washing it down with a swig of coffee, he said, "Besides, it doesn't match what she wrote on the wall. If this was about Zadock, wouldn't she have said 'give' him back, not 'bring' him back?"

Ortensi paused, a forkful of pancake halfway to his mouth. "Do you have another explanation, Mr. Strauss?"

"No," Henry forced out. "But it doesn't mean there isn't one. I propose we join the other searchers in the wood looking for the missing surveyor. If he was the victim of some ghostly attack, perhaps we might find some clue, either to his disappearance or to the haunting itself."

Ortensi gave him a rather patronizing smile. "I understand your eagerness, Mr. Strauss, but the wood is a vast place. If the other men looking for Mr. Norris can't find him, our group has little chance. Vincent, Elizabeth, and I are all creatures of the city and would be lucky not to lose ourselves. Unless you have some experience…?"

Henry ground his teeth together. "No. But the ghost originally haunted the wood. Perhaps she retreats there during the day? If we explore the ruined town, we might find something."

"There is little of it remaining at this point," Ortensi replied. "And I assure you, I made a thorough investigation of the area myself and sensed nothing. But perhaps your instruments might discover something I missed." He smiled. "Why don't you and your able assistant go to the construction site and take your readings? Vincent, Elizabeth, and I will remain here and concentrate on the ghost's appearances in the town."

Henry stiffened. Was Ortensi deliberately trying to separate them? But no, that was ridiculous. He should be grateful—the man offered him a chance to show his inventions could find a solution where traditional methods failed. "Yes…an excellent suggestion."

"I'll try automatic writing," Lizzie said. "As Rosanna seems eager to communicate with her words."

Ortensi held up his bandaged fingers. "I appreciate the thought, Elizabeth, and we may have to resort to it. But I'd prefer you not endanger yourself just yet. Why don't you use your psychometric gift on the wall where the ghost wrote instead? The hotelkeeper is quite eager to patch over it, but I talked him into waiting for my permission."

For a moment, Henry thought she'd argue. But she merely nodded. "Very well."

"As for you, Vincent," Ortensi went on, "last night's events have given me an idea. If you'll accompany me into the town, I'll explain it to you while we walk."

Henry wanted to demand he explain it immediately to all of them. But like Lizzie, Vincent only nodded.

Well. It was clear who gave the orders here, and who did not. Ortensi might be the most experienced among them—and the most famous—but did he have to assume they'd all jump to obey him?

Although given Lizzie and Vincent's behavior, the assumption was not without merit.

It hardly mattered. "Come along, Jo," Henry said, rising to his feet. Ortensi had given Henry the opportunity to prove himself, and Henry for one would not waste it. "Let us pay a call on the late Miss Rosanna at her home."

Vincent followed Sylvester out of the hotel and onto the streets of Devil's Walk. Such as they were—the place appeared to consist of nothing more than a single main street, intersected with a few smaller lanes, and interrupted by the square with the clock and moon towers. At least he didn't have to worry about getting lost here.

Henry getting lost in the woods was an entirely different concern. Why had Henry taken such an immediate dislike to Sylvester? Vincent had assumed his assurance of Sylvester's talent would be adequate to dispel whatever lingering paranoia Henry possessed when it came to mediums.

Perhaps it was nothing more than lack of sleep. After all, Henry had seemed his normal self in bed last night. Tender, in thought and deed. Asking after Vincent's health, worrying about him, as if Vincent in some way deserved to be fussed over.

"You seem troubled," Sylvester said.

Vincent stepped carefully around a patch of particularly wet-looking mud. There was little hope of preserving his shoes in a place like this, but at least he could keep from splashing anything onto his striped trousers. A silver-gray vest and bottle green cutaway completed his ensemble, a splash of color amidst the drab grayness of the town. "I'm only tired. Having to change rooms in the middle of the night because a ghost has broken one's window does tend to make for a restless sleep."

Sylvester tipped his hat to a woman sweeping off her stoop. "I imagine it does. I wonder why the ghost chose to manifest to you?"

"Hard to say." But it was a good question. "Perhaps it was random...but I wasn't alone."

Sylvester arched a brow. "Oh?" He lowered his voice. "I thought the young porter was making eyes at you. I take it I was correct."

Mediumistic talents occurred most often in women. There were also frequent cases such as Lizzie's, where biology made some error in the womb, causing a woman to be formed other than nature would otherwise have dictated. When mediums were male, there was a decided tendency for them to have the sort of sexual preferences of which society disapproved. Vincent had never spoken of his inclinations to Sylvester, but it hardly came as a surprise to find the older man guessed them easily enough.

The *who*, however, likely would come as a shock. "Henry was with me."

A carriage clattered past, and Vincent stepped hastily aside to keep it from splashing mud onto his trousers. When it passed, Sylvester gave Vincent a look of disbelief. "Surely you must be joking with me."

"Henry is a good man," Vincent protested. "I know he's been a bit short with you, but he has many fine qualities."

Sylvester shook his head wearily. "I'm certain he does. I'd wondered why you'd tie yourself to a crackpot."

"Henry isn't a crackpot!" Vincent stopped dead in his tracks. "I meant every word I said about his accomplishments, as did Lizzie. How could you imagine I'd—"

"Get back to work! Or so help me, I'll fire the lot of you!"

Vincent and Sylvester exchanged a startled glance. "That sounded like Mr. Emberey," Sylvester said. "Come on."

They found Emberey down one of the side streets, standing in front of a saloon, his hands on his hips. Despite the early hour, several men lazed about in front of the establishment, pints in their hands. Emberey's face flushed scarlet, his jaw clenching so hard Vincent worried his teeth might crack.

"Sorry, boss," one of the men said, although he didn't sound very sorry at all. "But we ain't going back. What good is pay if some damned ghost kills us all, like she did Norris?"

"Mr. Norris is merely missing," Emberey shot back.

"You can say what you like," the man replied. He leaned over and spat. "We ain't going back, not until the ghost is gone."

Emberey's fist curled, as if he wished to hit something. Or everything. "You are relieved of your position as foreman, Mr. Brooks. Retroactively. The pay owed you from last week will be docked to reflect it."

"What! That ain't fair!" Brooks sat up, knocking his pint over when he bumped the table. "I did the damned work, and you'll pay me for it in full!"

A dark rumble went through the crowd of men, and Vincent's muscles tensed as the mood shifted.

"Damned fool," Sylvester muttered. He left Vincent and strode toward the crowd. "Gentlemen!" he exclaimed, holding up his hands. "There's no need to quarrel."

Emberey shot him an angry look. "There's every need. Each day they don't work on the mill puts us farther behind schedule and costs Mr. Carlisle money."

"Of course, of course," Sylvester said with a placating smile. "But have no fears. My colleagues and I are working on a solution to our little ghost problem right now."

"Haven't done much so far," Brooks growled. He jerked his head in Vincent's direction. "And now you've brought in some fucking redskin?"

Vincent bit his tongue until he tasted blood, but said nothing. Thank God Henry wasn't here, or the whole affair would have turned into a brawl. One they had no hope of winning against a mob of angry men who worked their muscles for a living.

"No one can do anything," said an unfortunately familiar voice. Fitzwilliam had come up silently behind them.

This man had dared lay hands on Henry. Vincent itched to finish the fight he'd started last night. A low growl escaped him.

Fitzwilliam ignored him; his eyes fixed on Brooks. "This is the Lord's will," he proclaimed. "You will suffer for your sins."

"Get out of here, you drunk," shouted a man. Given he was drinking at ten o'clock in the morning, the accusation seemed rather hypocritical.

"You don't know anything." Fitzwilliam glowered at Brooks, but his words seemed aimed at them all. "My family descended from one of the children spared when the witch's ghost burned the old town. God shielded the innocents from her flame that night and let the guilty die in fire. And now once again God has sent the witch to do His work!" Fitzwilliam's eyes snapped suddenly to Vincent's face. "And any who oppose Him will feel His wrath."

"Five dollars to any man who removes him," Emberey said.

There came a wild scramble, chairs and tables overturning as the crowd surged forward. Vincent found himself shoved aside; he fell heavily to one knee in the mud.

Sylvester hauled him to his feet. "Are you all right, my boy?" he asked.

Vincent swiped at the mud on his trousers with his handkerchief. "Only my dignity is wounded. And my trousers."

There was no sign of Fitzwilliam, or the men chasing him. Vincent vindictively hoped he wouldn't get away entirely unscathed.

Emberey frowned at the overturned chairs. "Blast," he swore. Turning to Sylvester, he added, "Mr. Carlisle is paying for results, Ortensi. Time is money, after all."

Emberey stormed away. "What an utter ass," Vincent remarked, when he was well out of earshot.

"Quite." Sylvester shook his head. "But he's right, in his way. We should conclude this quickly, before the situation can escalate."

"Do you think Norris is dead?" Vincent asked quietly.

"I don't know." Sylvester started off, and Vincent fell in beside him. "Rosanna broke your window and left us a message last night, but she did nothing truly harmful."

"I had salt down."

Sylvester paused. "Salt? Why? If you suspected she'd appear—"

"Of course I didn't." Vincent's stomach did a slow roll. What if Sylvester turned against him? Thought Vincent paranoid…or worse. "I haven't slept without wards since Dunne died," he confessed quietly. "The ghost that killed him…it's still out there."

"I see." Sylvester's hand came to rest on his shoulder. "I'm sorry. Once we're finished here, I'll do anything I can to help you."

"I don't know if it has any interest in me," Vincent whispered. "But…it possessed me. That night. And it was too strong."

The silence between them was agony, each second like the flick of a knife on Vincent's skin. Then Sylvester's fingers tightened. "Ah, Vincent. I didn't realize. My poor boy."

Emotion constricted Vincent's throat and burned in his eyes. He forced it back—the open street wasn't the place to break down. "I…I didn't know how to tell you. I feared…"

"We'll speak of this later," Sylvester said gently. "But James would have been the first to forgive you."

"Lizzie said the same thing."

"I'm sure she did." Sylvester let his arm drop. "She'd also remind us we have business to attend to at the moment."

"Yes." Vincent tucked his muddy handkerchief away, wishing it clean enough to wipe his face. "You never said where we're going."

Sylvester offered him a sly smile. "Didn't I? We're going to look for answers."

Vincent quirked an eyebrow. "How very enlightening. And where are we going to find these answers?"

"Prepare your soul, Vincent." Sylvester clapped him on the shoulder. "We're going to church."

"Can we look more closely at the moon tower?" Jo asked Henry as they made their way out of Devil's Walk. The steel tower, perched as it was atop the clock tower, loomed over the entire town like an admonishing finger. Or something more phallic, as Vincent pointed out the night before.

Although he knew he ought to refuse—they had work to do—in truth Henry rather wanted to see it closer himself. "We can't take long," he admonished. "But we can at least peek into the workings."

The clock tower sat atop a large, rectangular building, which stood apart from the houses fronting the square. The door proved unlocked, the interior dim, and the air faintly musty. To one side, a set of metal stairs ran up past the inner workings of the clock, and presumably thence to the moon tower above.

"Look, Henry—is that the dynamo?" Jo asked excitedly.

"Indeed it is." He followed her at a more sedate pace. "The steam engine here turns the armature, which reacts to the magnets on the stator to generate electricity." Or it would, if Emberey bothered to have the arc lamp repaired. More lamps lined the ceiling of the interior, all of them cold and dark as the coal furnace.

"I wish we could see it in operation," she said, examining the stator.

"As do I." He shifted the pack on his back, which held their equipment. "But we have work, and we'd best get to it."

They left the town behind and made for the forest. It didn't take Henry long to appreciate the unease the workers reported feeling in Devil's Walk Woods. Even from a distance, the place seemed dark, a shadow on the landscape, bisected by the dull iron of the river. Seeing it close at hand did nothing to change his impression.

"Should we take measurements?" Jo asked. "As we go farther in toward the old town?"

He nodded. "An excellent idea, Jo. I should have thought of it myself."

She beamed at his praise. Henry slid his pack from his shoulders, wincing at a twinge in the left one, the old wound making its presence known. They measured temperature, barometric pressure, and magnetic field strength, before continuing on.

Fortunately, the company had put in a rail spur to move building materials and equipment to the construction site. It cut a wide path through the dense trees along the riverside, small trestles bridging the occasional ravine. Without it, Henry feared he would have become quickly lost in the tangle.

The woods appeared to have remained untouched since colonial times. The trees grew tall and thick, their canopies blotting out the sky. A sea of brown and gray trunks spread out on every side, made impenetrable by thickets of thorn and laurel. Water dripped from the leaves, and branches rubbed together in the wind, letting off low, eerie moans.

"I wonder how many of the frightening sounds the workers blamed on the ghost were just the trees," Jo remarked, the first time they heard a groan from above them.

"Let's hope most of them," he replied. "Even if the ghost is here, daylight will protect us. The most the ghost can do, even overcast as it is, is watch. Perhaps play with our perceptions in some minor way."

They stopped every fifteen minutes to take measurements. The forest lay eerily silent around them—no sound of birds or chatter of squirrels. Just the creaks of the trees and the mutter of river water over rock. After a few rounds of taking the pack off and putting it back on, the ache in Henry's shoulder went from intermittent to continuous.

Soon Jo outpaced him, her youth lending energy to her strides that his decidedly lacked. Even though the day wasn't unusually hot, it was still July, and a film of sweat covered his skin and stuck his clothes to him most uncomfortably. The grade was gentle but continuous, far more strenuous than the streets he normally walked, and the railroad ties seemed determined to trip him.

"Let's stop for a rest," he called.

Jo bounded back to him like a fawn. "Can we eat lunch?"

"It's not yet noon."

"I know, but I'm hungry. Please, Henry?"

It was emotional blackmail, but he couldn't help but give in when she turned those big eyes on him. "Oh, very well. I didn't have much breakfast and find I'm a bit peckish myself."

They settled on the massive trunk of one of the felled trees. Henry took a long, grateful drink from his canteen, while Jo unwrapped their sandwiches. "Why don't you like Mr. Ortensi?" she asked as she passed one to him.

This wasn't a conversation he wished to have. "I like him just fine."

Jo rolled her eyes as she took a bite out of her sandwich. Once she'd swallowed, she said, "No you don't. I just don't understand why. He seems so nice, and he's Vincent and Lizzie's friend."

Henry hesitated. What could he tell her? That he disliked Ortensi for the same reasons everyone else admired him? His fame, his connection with Vincent?

Should Henry confess he'd lied about the society's reception? Admit all these measurements he asked her to take might be for naught? Allow he might be making everything worse instead of better, despite his intentions?

He couldn't. Jo looked at him with such trust. She relied on him to keep her safe, to teach her as best he might, and hopefully prepare her for an independent life of her own someday. How could he tell her she might have made a grave error in placing her trust in him?

"I dislike the way Ortensi issues orders to the rest of us," he said, which was true as far as it went. "I know he was close to their mentor, but he *isn't* Dunne. Yet they accept his authority without question. I'd prefer if he would be a little less high-handed a bit more open to sharing his reasoning."

"Hmm." Jo narrowed her eyes but mercifully didn't say anything.

They finished their lunch in silence. Once they finished, Henry rested for a few minutes, while Jo poked about amidst the trees: inspecting leaves, measuring the girth of the trunks with her arms, and generally enjoying herself.

"Don't wander far," he warned.

"I won't, Henry," she said, her tone containing all the exasperation a sixteen-year-old could muster.

He shook his head. Had he been this confident at her age?

No, actually. Because by then, Isaac had absconded with all their money, breaking Henry's heart in the process. Henry and his mother moved from their stately home in the better part of Baltimore, to a one-room apartment whose shabby walls let in the winter wind. He'd been confused and hurt, and blamed himself for all that had happened.

Mother died before he reached his seventeenth birthday, victim to pneumonia brought on by the chill of their new lodgings. Father's death had left Henry the man of the family, and he'd failed in his most basic charge, to look after his mother.

He wouldn't let Jo down, as he had Mother. Wouldn't let Vincent and Lizzie down. Not again.

Jo returned, her yellow dress bright amidst the dreary mist that seemed to cling to the forest. Her life had too much tragedy in it for her few years, and the sight of her smile lifted his heart.

"Are you all right?" Jo asked, cocking her head to the side.

"Of course." He shouldered his pack again, grunting at the accompanying flare of pain. "Let's continue on. We can't be far from the ruins, certainly."

As he stood, a whisper of wind slipped through the trees, setting them to creaking. The breeze seemed to strengthen near the ground, and a zephyr of leaves rose up, uncovering the end of what appeared to be a wooden board.

The skin on Henry's neck pricked. He glanced at Jo, but she didn't seem to have noticed the breeze. As if had been meant only for him.

No, his imagination was running away with him. It was just an odd trick of weather. Still, he knelt to see what it had revealed.

"What's that?" Jo asked, peering over his shoulder.

"It looks to be a wooden plank." He brushed leaf mold from the weathered surface. "And there are words carved into it."

He tugged on the wood. The plank came free from the earth reluctantly, as though something held it back.

Maggots erupted from beneath it.

Henry shouted and dropped the plank. Crawling things filled the hole where it had lain, their fat, white bodies writhing in protest at the exposure to sunlight. His gorge rose, and he stepped back, bumping into Jo. The insects boiled out, thrashing blindly, some crawling along the exposed length of what proved to be a wooden signpost.

"Ew," Jo said, and bent to inspect them.

"Get away!" Henry pulled her back. His heart pounded against his ribs. The sudden sensation of someone watching swept over him.

"They're just maggots, Henry," she said in exasperation. "They can't hurt me."

"I don't care." Henry cast about, but the forest lay still around them. Nothing stirred.

And yet he couldn't shake the feeling unseen eyes peered from behind every tree.

He took a deep breath, fighting to steady his nerves. "Come along," he said. "Let's get to the ruins. There will be workers at the mill site." Getting out of these empty woods and to a place with other people seemed suddenly, desperately important.

"All right," she agreed doubtfully.

Henry returned to the tracks and set off at a brisk pace. And refused to look back, despite the sensation of something following on their heels.

CHAPTER 8

"**AND WHY** are we going to church?" Vincent asked as they approached the small wooden structure. "A sudden attack of piety?"

Sylvester chuckled. "It's not the church we're interested in, but rather those buried just outside it."

Vincent surveyed the graveyard, enclosed by an iron fence. "The villagers burned Rosanna, and even if chunks of bone remained, they must be at the ruins."

"Ah, but it isn't Rosanna we're looking for," Sylvester replied. "My hope is the vestry includes information on the reburials."

"What do you mean?"

Sylvester paused beside the cemetery gate. Peering inside, Vincent noticed a large number of freshly dug graves. Three no doubt belonged to the men killed in the wall collapse at the construction site, but there were far too many for even a rash of accidents to account for.

"The dead of Whispering Falls," Sylvester said, indicating the graves with a showman's flourish. "Removed from their rest amidst the forest and reburied here."

Vincent frowned. "Why?"

"My understanding is the new houses for the mill workers are to be built where the old church and cemetery stood." Sylvester shrugged. "At any rate, the graves would have been disturbed, so they were removed and reinterred here, in consecrated ground."

Vincent folded his arms and cocked his head to one side. "And this is relevant to Rosanna because...?"

"'Bring him back.'" Sylvester rested his hand lightly on the gate. "What if Zadock's bones now rest here, rather than in the forest?"

Could Sylvester be right? Had some obsessive jealousy lingered even beyond death, driving Rosanna to fury when her lover's bones were removed? "But the legend says the townsfolk fell on Rosanna immediately. Surely Zadock wouldn't have been buried so quickly. His body would still have been laid out."

"Your point is a valid one and may indeed prove the case." Sylvester let his hand fall and started for the church again. "But I sincerely doubt they dragged Rosanna away and set her aflame immediately, as the legend would have us believe. It takes time for such anger to erupt into violence. Drunken mutterings at a wake might turn deadly at the funeral itself. At any rate, we should be able to find out in the church."

Vincent followed him. "There's a record of who is buried in what grave, I take it?"

"Indeed. The tombstones were initially brought down along with the bodies, in hopes of being placed on the appropriate graves," Sylvester replied as he mounted the steps to the church doors. "But time had left so many cracked and worn, there was little to do but discard them. The tombstones are what alerted me to the reburial in the first place—I'd hardly stepped off the train before being confronted with the sight of broken slabs. Needless to say, I was somewhat alarmed, until Mr. Emberey explained what happened."

Sylvester rested his hand on the latch. "According to him, brass tags mark each of the new graves, and a list was compiled matching the numbers on the tags with the names of those buried beneath. I inquired whether there were any plans to replace the tags with more permanent markers. He said it would cost a great deal, and the company had no such intention."

"I'm shocked," Vincent muttered.

The door opened beneath Sylvester's hand. They entered the dark interior of the church, illuminated only by the weak sunlight streaming through the plain windows. The boards creaked beneath their shoes, and the air smelled of dust and the pages of the hymnals stacked on shelves to one side. Vincent followed Sylvester down the center aisle, past wooden pews polished to a sheen by the touch of generations of worshippers. A great wooden cross hung behind the pulpit; beneath it stood a small door.

"Ah, here we are," Sylvester said, opening the door. "The vestry, such as it is."

The space was indeed tiny, with barely enough room for a single bookshelf and desk. A spare set of vestments hung on a coat rack in one corner. Various ledgers crammed the shelves—accounts of births and deaths, no doubt. And hopefully reburials.

"It would be the newest, I should think," Sylvester muttered, half to himself.

Vincent scanned the shelves. One crumbling tome caught his eye, and he plucked it free. "Look—the parish records from Whispering Falls," he said in surprise.

"Curious. I wonder if the legend exaggerated the deaths, and the pastor survived. Or if his replacement ventured into the church to retrieve the records. It's one of the few structures the fire left more or less intact." Sylvester shook his head. "Either way, it doesn't matter to our current search."

"True enough." Vincent replaced the old book, looking for one much newer. "Is this it?"

Sylvester took the heavy tome from him and laid it open on the desk. Vincent peered over his shoulder as Sylvester flipped to the last set of entries. Thankfully, the parson wrote in a neat hand and kept meticulous records. "Names and birth and death dates. Perhaps he hopes the company might pay for tombstones after all. Let's see…Prudence, Hepzibah…ah." Sylvester tapped it. "Zadock. And it appears his death is the latest on record. This must be the man from the legend. He's here, and the ghost is drawn to his bones."

The deep roar of the falls was audible long before coming into sight. Soon the scent of raw earth and sap accompanied the sound, and Henry and Jo stepped out of the thick woods into what had once been the town of Whispering Falls.

Only a few weeks ago, the tangled woods had no doubt claimed this area. Now, the trees had been razed and signs of human activity lay all around. The ground was torn apart in many places, the brown soil heaved up where the stumps of mighty trees had been wrenched free. Several flat cars sat at the end of the rail spur, waiting to be unloaded. The foundations of the mill lay near the falls. Walls rose up on three sides, only about ten feet in height so far. One corner and much of the fourth side were ragged and uneven; no doubt this was the wall that collapsed onto the workers and killed them.

To the west lay what yet remained of the old town. The ruins of a stone church still stood there, and Henry wondered if religious feeling had caused the men to leave its demolition until the last.

Near to it stood the jagged remains of the original buildings, their foundation stones blackened by century-old fire. The ruins gave way to rubble, then to bare earth, where work crews had cleared the eastern half of the town already.

Work crews who were conspicuously absent today. The silence lying over the old town was as deep as that of the forest.

"Where is everyone?" Jo asked, her voice slightly hushed.

"I…I don't know." Henry cast about uneasily. The only movement came from the falls. Water, churned white, leapt and danced over rocks as it poured from a high promontory, tossing up a shimmer of mist at the base. Worn brown stones showed through the spray here and there.

"Perhaps they've gone on strike due to the ghost," he reasoned. "Or perhaps they're all out searching for the missing surveyor. Norris."

"Wouldn't we have heard them calling for him?"

Jo had a point. "Whatever the reason, we have the site to ourselves today," he said, and tried not to shiver. It was broad daylight, after all. "This is good, actually. We won't have to worry about convincing some foreman to stop work long enough to let us take measurements."

"True." She contemplated the ruins. "Where shall we start?"

Henry longed to investigate the new construction further. Not the mill as such, but rather the beginnings of the electrical plant that would be powered by the falls. From a distance, it appeared as if only the foundation had been poured, the sluiceways still under construction. The dynamos weren't yet on site, which was something of a disappointment.

Rosanna likely wouldn't haunt the new buildings, though. "Let's go to the church and take readings there," he said reluctantly. "After we've canvassed the area, we'll move into the remaining ruins. With any luck, we'll find something instructive to take back with us."

"And impress Mr. Ortensi?" Jo asked with a lifted brow.

It wasn't Ortensi he needed to impress. But Henry couldn't say that without betraying himself, so he merely gave her a quelling frown.

They worked steadily, losing track of time in favor of scientific zeal. Unfortunately, none of the results seemed particularly conclusive. The temperature was lower inside the church—but it was a shady area whose stone walls would warm more slowly than the air outside. The readings of the portable galvanometer fluctuated wildly, but, as Henry had confessed to Vincent the night before, he had no real idea what they meant. How high would a reading have to be to indicate a ghostly presence? Might there be iron or some other element in the soil affecting the electromagnetic fields? He didn't know.

Still, he tried to retain a cheerful demeanor for Jo's sake. When they took the last of their measurements, he rose to his feet with a groan. So intent had he been on the task, he hadn't even noticed the discomfort in his joints from all the kneeling and bending over.

Another discomfort also made itself known. "Excuse me for a moment, Jo," he said, making a vague gesture toward the woods. She seemed to take his meaning, because she only said, "I'm going to draw a rough map and mark the differences in readings on it. Perhaps there's a pattern."

"Excellent idea." He touched her shoulder and received a pleased grin in return.

Henry made his way through the wide swath of cleared land and ducked into the forest. The trees towered above him, their canopy blocking the thin sunlight and casting the forest floor into near darkness. A rough path, perhaps made by deer, cut through laurel thickets. Their branches snagged his clothes as he ducked between them. When he was certain of his privacy, he unfastened his trousers and attended to matters. Once again in order, he turned to go back the way he'd come.

The path behind him had vanished.

"Any luck?" Lizzie asked by way of greeting, when Vincent and Sylvester returned to the hotel. She sat in the parlor, sipping lemonade and reading the newspaper. A worn Bible sat on the table in front of her.

"Perhaps." Sylvester told her of their finding at the church. When he finished, she nodded her head slowly.

"It sounds plausible," she agreed.

Vincent had slipped into the chair beside her. Now he leaned back, folding his hands over his stomach. "And you? Did your psychometry tell you anything?"

"Nothing we didn't already know. The ghost is angry. Furious." She pursed her lips. "But while you two were sullying hallowed grounds with your presence, I paid a visit to Mr. and Mrs. Norris, the parents of the missing surveyor."

Sylvester sat at the head of the table. "Why?"

"I told them I might be able to find out what happened to their son, if they could give me anything of his to use my abilities on." She rested her fingers on the book. "They gave me his Bible—apparently he read from it every evening, so there should be a strong connection."

"Brilliant." Sylvester smiled.

Vincent let the front legs of his chair meet the floor with a thump. "Only if he's already dead. Psychometry won't let you contact the spirit of a living man."

"Yes, well, I didn't tell them that." Lizzie shrugged. "If I can't summon him, I'll return the Bible and say my only impression is that he yet lives. And if I can…at least they'll know the truth."

She had a point. "We can't do anything until Henry returns anyway. Let's see if we can make contact," Vincent agreed.

Unlike a true séance, Lizzie's psychometry didn't summon the spirit to manifest, so a darkened room wasn't necessary. Vincent fetched paper and pen, then settled at the table across from Lizzie while Sylvester looked on.

"Whenever you're ready," he said, pen poised to take note of any impressions she might receive.

Lizzie rested her hands on Norris's Bible. She glanced at Vincent, then took a deep breath and shut her eyes. The distant sounds of the hotel staff filtered through the closed door. A horse whinnied somewhere out on the street, and there came a muffled shout. The summer air hung close and still, and a drop of sweat made its way down Vincent's spine.

Lizzie's lips drew back in a grimace, tight against her teeth. "Trees," she said. "Trees all around. Where am I?"

Sylvester let out a soft sigh. Curse it all—Norris was dead, then, and not just missing.

"Trees," Lizzie repeated. "I—he—can't find his way out. There's something behind him. Pain—fire—"

She jerked back with a gasp, eyes flying open. Sylvester reached for her. "Lizzie? Lizzie, are you all right?"

She swallowed convulsively. "I…I think so." Vincent pushed her lemonade closer to her, and she took it gratefully. "Thank you, Vincent."

"What happened?" Sylvester leaned closer. "What did you see? Was Norris alone?"

"No." She shook her head. "That is—he was at first. In the forest. He lost his way."

"Not much of a recommendation for his skills as a surveyor," Vincent said.

Lizzie shook her head, a golden curl slipping over her shoulder. "It was brief, but I had the impression something was wrong. He *shouldn't* have been lost."

"The ghost's influence?" Sylvester asked.

"I think so. It wasn't sundown yet, but he couldn't find the way out. Then the sun set." She drained the rest of the lemonade from the glass. "And after that...fire."

"Oh hell." Vincent shoved his chair back, his heart suddenly knocking against his ribs. "Henry and Jo. They're in the woods, alone."

Henry blinked. He must have mistaken things. The deer trail was still there, it simply appeared different from this angle. Some of the branches he'd pushed through must have sprung back together.

He tried to find a break in the laurel. The bushes' twisted branches seemed suddenly sinister, contorted as though in a pose of silent agony, like the forest of suicides in Dante's hell. They clutched at one another, refusing to let him through.

He took a deep breath and ordered his heartbeat to slow. It was just some quirk of how the foliage grew. He'd find his way through in a moment.

"Henry," called a faint voice from deeper in the forest.

"Jo?" he yelled back. "Jo, is that you?"

"Henry," the voice said again, even fainter this time.

Why had Jo come into the woods? Did something frighten her in the old town, badly enough for her to seek him out?

Blast it. "Jo!" he shouted. "Where are you?"

No answer. He listened intently. There was no sound other than his own breath. No birds. No squirrels. Not even the groan of trees in the wind.

Now deeply worried, he started in the direction the call came from. "Jo? Jo! Answer me!"

The trees seemed to crowd in closer the farther he went. Branches scraped at his hands, and damp leaves clung to his face. The faint smell of burning stained the air.

Some trick of the wind must have carried the smoke of a hearth here. Someone in Devil's Walk still employed a wood stove for cooking rather than a coal or gas one. That must be it.

A clearing opened up before him, almost unnaturally circular in shape. The trees leaned in around the empty space, like silent spectators. Henry stepped into it, his heart beating at the base of his throat.

A flicker of movement caught his eye, and he spun. "Jo?"

"Henry," said the voice, but no longer distant. This time he heard the crackle of burning wood, the snap of bones bursting from the heat.

This time, it came from right over his shoulder.

Vincent stumbled to a halt at the edge of the site of the new mill, gasping for breath. He'd run as fast as he could from the town—although given how seldom he ran anywhere, it hadn't been nearly as fast as he would have liked.

"Henry?" he shouted. "Jo?"

The roar of the waterfall swallowed his words. He cast about, but saw only the stumps of walls, the flat cars laden with supplies, and the detritus left behind by the workers.

"Henry!" His throat ached with the force of his shout. "Jo! Where are you?"

"Vincent?" Jo's voice, thank God. A moment later, she raced into view from the older ruins, her skirts hiked up to let her run. "Vincent!"

Oh hell. He caught her by the arms when she ran up to him. "Where's Henry?"

Her eyes were wide with fear. "He went into the woods to..." she gestured vaguely.

Piss, she no doubt meant. "And?"

"He hasn't come back." She gripped Vincent's arm in turn, fingers digging in through his coat. "I called for him and he hasn't answered!"

Vincent bit back an oath, even as fear choked his veins with ice. "Do you know where he entered the woods?"

"Not exactly." She glanced down. "I didn't watch him leave."

"The general area, then?"

She gestured to the southeastern edge of forest. It looked rather formidably dense, and he didn't bother to hold back his curse this time.

"He's in trouble, isn't he?" Her voice shook with terror.

"I don't know." He tried to project calm for her sake, although it was probably too late for that. "This is Henry we're talking about. He probably just got...got interested in something scientific. A rock, maybe."

"You can find him, can't you?" Her fingers tightened on his forearm, hard enough to leave bruises. "You're an Indian—can't you track him?"

"Jo. I spent my entire life in Manhattan before moving to Baltimore." Vincent stared at the forbidding edge of the forest, which would have been worrisome even if there wasn't an angry ghost in the mix. "The sum total of my knowledge is that woods are filled with bugs, snakes, trees, and probably bears, and that I don't want to have anything to do with them." He released his hold on her. "But as Henry's seen fit to get himself lost, it would seem I have no choice."

Because Henry was just lost, that was all. The sun was still high in the sky. Henry had just gotten himself turned around, and he wasn't going to end up like Norris, dead and rotting God only knew where amidst the trees.

"I'll come with you," Jo offered.

"No." Vincent pulled free from her grasp. "Stay here. *Don't* leave this spot, no matter what, not even if you hear Henry and I both calling to you. It won't be us, I promise. Now, do you have a watch? Good. If we're not back within two hours, return to Devil's Walk and tell Sylvester."

She bit her lip. "But…"

"No." He gripped her shoulder briefly with one hand. "With any luck, Henry just got turned around, and we'll be back in a few minutes. But if there are otherworldly forces at work here, letting Sylvester and Lizzie know as soon as possible will make all the difference. Do you understand?"

He hated the fear creeping back into her eyes, eclipsing the momentary hope his presence gave her. "I-I do. Be careful."

"I will." He let go of her and turned to the woods.

The trees became no more welcoming the closer he approached. He scanned the ground—perhaps some latent ability to track, hidden deep in his blood, would appear?

It didn't, of course. He stopped at the edge of the forest, breathing deeply. The air smelled of raw earth and the sap of massacred trees. No animals stirred, although perhaps that was ordinary for this time of day? He hadn't the slightest idea.

Neither did Henry, most likely. Henry, who had vanished just like Norris.

Blast Henry. What if Vincent couldn't find him? What if the minutes turned into hours, then into days, just as they had for Norris's family? What if it was Henry's belongings Lizzie went through next, his last moments she reported?

Vincent clenched his jaw. It wouldn't happen. He couldn't bear it.

"Henry!" he called. "I'm coming for you!" And plunged into the woods.

CHAPTER 9

HENRY RAN.

Terror lent him speed. He didn't dare look over his shoulder, too afraid of what he might see. Branches whipped across his face, nearly tearing his spectacles free. His shoe caught on a root, and he almost pitched forward, barely catching himself on the tree it belonged to.

Leaves crunched beneath his feet. His breath scraped in his throat, too loud for him to hear whether anything gave pursuit. Any moment, he expected to feel a skeletal hand grab the back of his coat, or a blast of cold against his neck. His lungs burned and his sides ached, but he didn't dare stop.

The trees fell abruptly away—thank heavens, he'd made it back to the construction site.

Except there was no large expanse of raw earth and half-built walls. Just trees, outlining a clearing in an eerily perfect circle.

Damn it. He'd gotten turned around and ended up where he began. If only he hadn't left the compass with Jo, but he'd hardly imagined he'd need it. Barely breaking stride, he raced back into the trees. He'd make certain he went in a straight line this time. Eventually it would take him back to the work site, or the railroad tracks. Anywhere these accursed trees didn't hem him in.

He ducked, dodged beneath branches, jumped a small gully, and—

Found himself back in the clearing again.

"No," he said aloud. It wasn't possible. He *knew* he'd gone, if not in a straight line, at least not in a circle.

The ghost wanted him here and didn't intend to let him leave.

"Henry!"

A shriek escaped Henry, and he spun, hands up to fight off whatever horror had come upon him.

Vincent caught his wrists. "Henry, stop, it's me!"

Relief weakened Henry's legs. "Dear lord, don't do that again!" he gasped. "You nearly gave me apoplexy."

Vincent pulled him close. "Thank God you're all right."

"I...yes. I'm fine." But he must have sounded as shaky as he felt, because Vincent tightened his arms convulsively.

"I've got you, sweetheart." Vincent whispered against his sweaty hair. "Tell me what happened."

When Henry finished, Vincent caught his chin and tipped his head back. "I'm glad you're all right," he said, and kissed Henry tenderly.

Henry knew he must reek of sweat after his frantic run, but if Vincent didn't care, neither did he. Just the taste of Vincent's mouth, cinnamon cachous and faded coffee, calmed his racing heart.

"Thank you," he managed, when the kiss ended. "Not to sound ungrateful, but what are you doing here?"

"Lizzie convinced Norris's parents to lend her one of his possessions." Vincent sighed and ran his hands lightly up and down Henry's arms. "He's dead. He died here in the woods, disoriented, attacked by the ghost. And I...I panicked."

Not good news. Even so, Henry said, "Vincent Night, panic?"

Vincent's dark eyes remained sober. "Yes. I was terrified the same fate might have befallen you and Jo. When Jo said you'd gone into the woods and not returned..." He took a deep breath, and the faintest hint of his usual smile touched his lips. "At first I thought I'd have no hope of finding you amidst the trees, but fortunately I heard you crashing about like an elephant in a glassworks."

Of course Vincent would have worried for them...and yet hearing it out loud sent a foolish warmth through Henry's chest. "I'm glad you came along when you did," he admitted. "If you hadn't..."

"I don't think Rosanna could have done you any real harm, not during the day," Vincent replied. "Just play nasty little tricks to frighten you and keep you disoriented."

"And my fear gave her energy to continue." Henry had stupidly lost his head—he should have stayed and confronted the spirit. Instead he'd panicked. What must Vincent think of him?

"It is odd she kept directing you back here." Vincent let go of Henry and stepped back. "The clearing doesn't seem entirely natural, does it? Too free of undergrowth in just this area. And—what's that?"

Henry turned. Burned into the bark of the nearest trunk was the letter H.

"The devil?" Curse it, if only he had his instruments with him. He bent over to inspect it more closely and spotted another letter on the trunk behind it.

"There's more," he said.

Vincent started forward, but Henry held up his hand. "Wait." He stepped back again, shifting for a better angle.

In the right line of sight, the letters spilled across the trunks. "H-E-L-P-M-E," he read. "Help me?"

Vincent met his gaze, looking equally puzzled. "So it would seem. But what could it mean? It doesn't make any—"

There came a loud creak from the branches above them. Startled, Henry looked up in time to see something plummeting toward them.

He leapt back with a cry, dragging Vincent with him. The object smashed into the ground barely a foot away, releasing a stench of burned pork and rotting flesh so powerful Henry choked on the bile rushing into his throat.

A man's body lay there, twisted and broken from its fall. Blackened skin covered the charred features, arms drawn up in a pugilist's pose, mouth gaping in a silent scream.

Vincent gripped Henry's arm, but his eyes remained fixed on the body. He swallowed convulsively, and his voice grated when he said, "I think we've found Mr. Norris."

Some hours later, they sat around the table of the private parlor once again. Henry sipped a cup of weak tea, hoping to settle his nerves. The sight of the surveyor's charred body seemed inscribed on the inside of his eyelids, and the memory of the stench clogged his nose.

"A group of men have gone to retrieve the body," Ortensi said gravely. "Norris's father among them, to see if he can recognize the clothing, or whatever is left of it. But after Lizzie's earlier contact with Norris's spirit, there seems little doubt as to the victim's identity."

"Or how he died," Vincent said. He took his flask from his pocket and added a generous dollop to his coffee.

"I've already had a note from Mr. Emberey." Ortensi sat back in his chair, lacing his hands in front of him. "He wants results. Now. Otherwise, he fears there will be a panic."

"I can't say I disagree with his assessment," Lizzie said.

Ortensi nodded. "What of your expedition into the woods, Mr. Strauss? Before discovering the body, I mean. Did your instruments detect anything useful?"

"No," Henry muttered. So much for returning in triumph. Instead, he'd returned thoroughly shaken.

"I see." Ortensi didn't smile, but Henry thought he detected smugness in the man's tone. "Fortunately Vincent and I had a productive morning."

After the grisly discovery, Henry hadn't even thought to ask. "Oh?"

"The bodies from the old cemetery were moved, and Zadock—Rosanna's lover—is buried here," Vincent said, but his brow furrowed as he spoke. "We speculate she referred to Zadock's bones when she wrote 'bring him back.' But with this new message, I'm no longer certain."

"'Help me,'" Lizzie murmured, frowning at her coffee.

Jo looked from one to the next of them. "Why would a ghost need help? Is she trapped here somehow? On this side of the veil, I mean?"

"It is a quandary," Ortensi said. "Perhaps she wished Mr. Strauss's help in returning Zadock's bones?"

"You're fitting the evidence to your preconceptions," Henry said, peeved despite himself.

Ortensi arched a brow. "Do you have a better theory? Please, share it with us."

"Maybe it wasn't Rosanna this time," Jo suggested. "Could the message have been from Mr. Norris? Maybe she's holding his ghost to this world, like in Reyhome Castle?"

Lizzie shook her head. "I sensed nothing of the sort."

"Oh." Jo deflated.

"Given what has happened, and the success of my attempt at psychometry, I say we cease speculating and ask Rosanna what she wants directly," Lizzie said. "As she seems eager to communicate through writing, we'll hold a séance and I'll—"

"Absolutely not!" Vincent exclaimed. "Look at what happened to Sylvester's hands. Worse—what happened to Norris. You'd be killed for certain."

"You don't know that," Lizzie replied. "And I'll thank you not to take such an imperious tone with me again."

Ortensi chewed on his lower lip. "Any medium will be in danger, but we must do something. One of us will have to channel her sooner or later."

"No, you won't." Henry's heart beat faster. "We can use the Electro-Séance."

Ortensi stared at him, as if he'd said something mad. "Electro... Séance? Really, Mr. Strauss—"

"No, wait, Henry's right." Vincent sat forward in his chair. "The Wimshurst machine will provide her the energy to manifest without a circle."

"She doesn't need a circle to manifest now," Ortensi replied, annoyance creeping into his tone.

"No, but without a séance, we have no control over *where* she appears." Excitement for the plan unfolding in his head flooded through Henry. "Surely she'd be drawn to an easily accessible source of energy like the Wimshurst machine. And once she manifests, we trap her inside the phantom fence."

"The phantom fence," Ortensi repeated in disbelief.

Henry forged on. "It uses the principles of electromagnetism to keep spirits out—or in. If we wish to be doubly sure of Rosanna manifesting where we wish, we could set our trap in the churchyard, where her lover's remains lie. If you're right about her wanting his bones, then his grave and the Wimshurst machine together will offer a potent lure. When she enters the interior of the fenced area, we connect the batteries and trap her there. I'll have the ghost grounder on hand, and—"

"Really, Mr. Strauss," Ortensi said, "it sounds as if you're trying to sell us some sort of patent medicine."

Henry's cheeks burned. "I had ad copy in mind when I devised the names, yes," he admitted. "But they work."

"I assure you, Sylvester, the machines are quite effective," Vincent said.

"When they don't backfire and give the ghost more energy to attack us," Lizzie added wryly.

"It only happened once!" Henry protested. "This will be different." It had to be.

Ortensi contemplated Vincent and Lizzie. "You think Mr. Strauss's plan will work?"

"Yes," Lizzie said. "I do." Vincent nodded as well.

"Very well." Ortensi settled back. "I suggest we work quickly. It would be best to have everything in place and ready by sundown."

~ * ~

"May I speak to you privately, Vincent?" Sylvester asked.

They stood outside the cemetery, the low sun casting their shadows ahead of them. Inside, Henry and Jo busied themselves setting up the phantom fence, ghost grounder, and other equipment. Lizzie opted to remain back at the hotel until closer to sunset, while Vincent and Sylvester helped Henry carry his devices to the graveyard. With that task done, there remained little for the two mediums to do save wait.

"Of course," Vincent replied. Turning back to the cemetery, he called, "We're going for a stroll, but we'll return shortly."

Henry waved a hand to indicate he'd heard. Vincent followed Sylvester away from the cemetery and back through the town. Norris's body had been returned to Devil's Walk, although its condition meant it lay in the receiving tomb rather than in his parents' parlor. No doubt it would remain there until the local pastor returned from the other communities in his charge.

Would there be a wake tonight? Given the nearly deserted streets, Vincent doubted it. No one seemed to want to venture outside even in the daylight. Even most of the shops were already shuttered.

"What did you wish to speak of?" he prompted, when Sylvester remained silent.

Sylvester sighed. He'd removed the bandages from his hands, although the skin was still pinker than usual. "You weren't with Mr. Strauss during his encounter with the ghost earlier today, correct?"

"No," Vincent said. "Why?"

"There's no easy way to say this, but…are you certain it wasn't a hoax on Mr. Strauss's part?"

Vincent came to a halt. "Of course! Henry hates such fakery more than anyone I've ever met. He'd never make up such a tale. Why would you even suggest it?"

"I mean no disrespect," Sylvester said hastily. "But the message. 'Help me.' Doesn't it strike you as…odd? As Miss Strauss said, what does a ghost have to fear?"

Vincent tensed. Taking a deep breath, he pulled back his temper. Sylvester didn't know Henry, didn't realize how good and honest he was. "Surely you don't mean to suggest Henry just happened to set up a hoax in the exact place Mr. Norris's body was concealed."

"Perhaps he spotted it hanging in the tree canopy?" Sylvester replied with a shrug. "I don't know, Vincent, and surely I'm wrong. The entire incident simply strikes me as strange, that's all."

"I don't understand." Vincent glanced back at the distant iron fence of the cemetery. "You seem determined not to trust Henry. I thought it was simply the unfamiliarity of his devices, but there's more, isn't there?"

"I've traveled the world. Performed in front of kings, yes, but also investigated ancient ruins and sought out half-forgotten tribes. My life has been saved by guides and interpreters, or put in peril by unscrupulous innkeepers willing to murder for a pocket watch." Sylvester shook his head. "The very fact I've lived to tell you this is proof I've honed my instincts to a sharper point than most. And every instinct I have says your Mr. Strauss is lying about something."

"In this case, your instincts are wrong." Vincent crossed his arms over his chest. "Henry is the most honest man I've ever met. Or...or perhaps what you sense as a falsehood is merely his concealment of my role in his life, which of course must be kept secret by its very nature."

"And what is your role in Mr. Strauss's life?" Sylvester cast him a look that held a trace of pity. "What is it *really?* He has ambitions, Vincent. I can tell. And ambitious men will leave others behind when they're of no more use."

"Henry would never do such a thing," Vincent insisted.

Sylvester didn't argue. "Perhaps we should return to the graveyard and see if our assistance is required."

"Yes," Vincent agreed.

Sylvester didn't know Henry, that was all. Yes, Henry had ambitions, but it didn't mean he'd leave Vincent behind.

The Psychical Society had already turned Vincent away thanks to his Indian blood. Vincent had assumed Henry would clash with the society if he found out...but what if that wasn't the case? What if he already knew? If the president mentioned it the other night, perhaps after Henry's lecture?

Henry dreamed of the sort of life Sylvester lived—world tours, his name in fifty-point type in the newspapers, the adulation of the masses. But he'd gone into business with an Indian and a woman who couldn't risk seeking out the limelight, as Sylvester put it.

Had he realized his mistake? Even if no one at the society brought up Vincent's rejected application, Henry was no fool. He could see the posters and newspaper articles as well as anyone. Famous mediums were always white, and often female. After the heady first days of their relationship, had he begun to view Vincent as a liability?

No. No, this was foolish. Sylvester was wrong. Vincent knew Henry, and Sylvester didn't. Yes, Sylvester had excellent instincts under ordinary circumstances. But Henry's unorthodox approach to the spirit world put him off, and it colored his normally good judgment.

That was all. And if not…Vincent would deal with it when it came.

Henry stood in the growing darkness amidst the graveyard, trying to keep his hands from shaking.

This would work. It must work. He'd capture Rosanna, drain her energy, and let the mediums step in to send her to the other side once and for all.

They'd go back to the hotel, have a celebratory dinner. He'd admit the Psychical Society rejected him. Lizzie would deride the society as fools, and Vincent forgive Henry for his harmless deception. Tomorrow they'd all go back to Baltimore, and he and Vincent would fall asleep in each other's arms until dawn. Ortensi would leave for Europe, and everything would be fine.

Absolutely fine.

"You set up Franklin bells at the cemetery entrance, I noticed," Lizzie remarked. She wore a dark blue dress and hat, a veil drawn across her features.

Henry nodded. "There's another, further along the street as well. I thought they might give us warning."

The cemetery gates stood wide, breaking the line of iron laid protectively around the graves inside. Thank heavens the local pastor was at one of his other parishes this week. Henry wouldn't have liked explaining their actions to a man of the cloth, who might be less than sanguine about them setting up their equipment on top of Zadock's grave. The Wimshurst machine sat on a folding table, as did the piezoelectric dispeller. A pile of salt covered the battery waiting to be hooked up to the dispeller, to prevent Rosanna from draining its energy. The copper wires of the phantom fence formed a loose circle around the grave. A small gap would let Henry pass in and out of the fence.

Ortensi stared at the arrangement rather skeptically, but said nothing. Henry's spine stiffened beneath his judging gaze. It didn't matter what the man thought. Soon enough, he'd see Henry's true mettle.

A beam of light cut through the darkness, where Jo waited among the graves, a short distance away from the phantom fence. Jo had asked to try out her new headlamp. Wires connected the arc lamp on the front of the headband to the heavy batteries inside a pack strapped to her back. Salt encased the batteries to keep them safe.

"How is the headlamp?" he called.

"Hot," came her reply. "But it works!"

"So I see."

"Are you ready?" Vincent asked.

Henry drew a deep breath. The warm summer air lay damp against his skin, and not even a breeze stirred.

"I'm ready," he said, and stepped into the circle of the phantom fence.

"Are you sure you don't want me to help?" Jo asked. "I can turn the crank and leave you free to use the ghost grounder."

"No." Henry picked up a heavy rubber glove and placed it on his left hand. Normally he'd hold the ghost grounder in his right, but the injury to his left shoulder would never let him turn the crank on the Wimshurst machine with his off hand. The ghost grounder itself—a simple copper rod, connected to a wire grounded to an iron rod he'd driven into the earth just outside the fence—lay waiting beside the dispeller. "This will be dangerous enough with only one of us inside the fence."

"Henry," Vincent started, then stopped.

The concern embodied in the single word warmed Henry's heart. "I'll be fine," he told Vincent. "Now, let's begin."

He went to the Wimshurst machine and began to turn the crank. The brushes ticked past one another, and a loud crack sounded as they discharged. Ortensi jumped at the sound, and it was all Henry could do to suppress a smile.

Hoping the charge was adequate, Henry said, "Now, Vincent."

Vincent's voice rang authoritatively through the graveyard. "We wish to make contact with the spirit of Rosanna," he said. "Spirit of Rosanna, use the energy provided by this machine and reveal yourself to us!"

The first set of Franklin bells began to ring.

Henry's heart beat faster, but he continued to turn the crank.

The second set, just within the cemetery gates, clanged to life.

"She's here," Vincent said, and the flame of the lantern in his hand went from bright orange to sickly blue.

The air around Henry grew colder and colder. The galvanometer went mad, registering a spike of electromagnetic energy, and another—then the hand remained pressed to the maximum side of the dial.

His breath caught in his lungs. She must be right on top of him.

Something flickered beside the table. A hint of flame. The edge of a dress.

Then she was there, just inches away. Her cooked-egg eyes stared into his, and the roasted meat of her face cracked as she lunged for him.

CHAPTER 10

"HENRY!" VINCENT shouted.

Henry leapt back, the ghost grounder already in his left hand. He thrust it out like a fencer, skewering Rosanna where her heart would have been. She jerked to a halt, and a shriek like the breaking of a thousand windows split the night.

"The dispeller!" Henry cried.

Curse it—Henry couldn't reach the dispeller and hold off Rosanna at the same time. Ignoring Sylvester's warning shout, Vincent slid through the gap in the phantom fence and dove for the table. The icy cold air made his fingers clumsy as he attached the wires, but at least the water inside hadn't frozen.

A moment later, a fine mist rose into the air from the dispeller. "That's it!" Henry shouted. Rosanna shrieked again, but the sound lacked the same violence. "Now go!"

Vincent went, Henry directly behind him. As soon as Vincent was out, Henry halted in the gap in the fence. "Jo—the fence!"

She connected the battery. Now trapped inside the fence, the ghost writhed, the flames of her hair and dress seeming to fade.

"Rosanna," Vincent said. The amulet would prevent any ghost from possessing him, but it didn't sever his connection with the otherworld. It wasn't the same as channeling, but he might be able to force her to listen to him. "Leave this place. Those who wronged you are long dead. They can't hurt you any more. They have found peace, a peace you deserve as well."

"We're trying to help you, as you wanted," Henry added. "Leave this place and find your rest, just as Zadock has found his."

She howled in rage, like the roar from a furnace door, suddenly opened. The flames enshrouding her blazed, as she directed all her remaining energy into them. A wall of heat struck Vincent, as if he stood inches from a roaring bonfire. The copper rod flared red hot, and the stench of burning rubber filled the air.

Henry let out a cry of pain, and the grounder fell from his hand. He staggered back, stripping off the smoking rubber glove and flinging it away.

Sylvester appeared on the other side of the phantom fence, his face lit by fire. "Begone, spirit!" he boomed, the force of his command like a strong wind against Vincent's skin. "Leave this place, and trouble those here no more!"

Lizzie appeared at Vincent's elbow, her face pale but calm. "Begone, spirit," she said with Sylvester, as he began again. Vincent hastily added his voice to hers, turning all of his will on the spirit trapped within the fence.

The mist from the dispeller ceased, its battery dead or its water boiled away by the heat of the ghost's rage. A horrible look of triumph twisted her charred features, and fear slicked Vincent's spine. With all the malevolent will of the dangerous dead, she reached out and deliberately grasped the copper wire of the fence with her hands.

It took only an instant. The copper glowed hot, but this was no sturdy rod, but merely a thin strand. It sagged, melted…and broke.

Before Vincent could react, she exploded outward, shrieking her fury. The temperature went from furnace hot to winter cold in a second as the ghost sucked every particle of available energy from the air around her.

The hem of Lizzie's dress burst into flame.

"Lizzie!" Vincent shouted, and ran to her with a wild idea of smothering the flames with his coat. But before he took another step, Rosanna's heat-shriveled hand struck his chest.

All the air burst from his lungs, and for a moment his feet left the ground. Then his back and skull collided with something hard and unyielding. The flames and frantic screams grew farther and farther away, until they vanished in darkness.

~ * ~

Vincent crumpled to the base of one of the oaks, like a thrown rag doll. Henry waited for him to twitch, to get up, to do anything but lie there motionless. The seconds ticked by, each one stretching into an eternity, and no, Vincent couldn't be dead, because that would mean the whole universe would go dark forever.

Vincent's eyelids fluttered.

The world snapped back into focus, even as relief stole the strength from Henry's knees. Heat brushed his skin, and he turned from Vincent to see Rosanna advancing on Jo and Lizzie. Jo's hands were full of loose dirt from one of the newly dug graves, and she heaped it atop Lizzie's skirts to smother the flames.

"Jo!" Henry shouted a warning.

She looked up, the bright beam of her headlamp cutting the darkness. Rosanna seemed to flicker and pale. Then Ortensi appeared in the light and flung a handful of salt straight into Rosanna's face.

"Be gone, spirit, and trouble us no more!" he thundered.

She flickered again, the beam of light showing through her as she grew less substantial. Henry's ears popped, and she vanished.

"Elizabeth!" Ortensi exclaimed. "Are you all right?"

"I'm fine, thanks to Jo's quick thinking." She held out her hand and let Ortensi help her to her feet, graveyard dirt sloughing from her skirts as she rose.

Henry ran to Vincent's side. Vincent struggled to sit up, but still looked dazed from his impact with the old oak. Henry dropped to his knees, his hands trembling. "Vincent? Are you all right?"

Vincent winced and put his hand to the back of his head. "What happened?"

"The ghost struck you."

He started to shake his head, then stopped. "I don't remember."

"We should get him to the doctor," Ortensi said, joining them.

"Agreed." Ignoring Vincent's protests, Henry hauled an arm over his shoulders, while Ortensi took the other.

"Should we come?" Lizzie asked anxiously.

"I don't think it will be necessary," Ortensi replied. "You should probably retire to the hotel. Miss Strauss, can you clean up this…mess?"

Henry surveyed the graveyard. The wires on the phantom fence sagged. The dispeller sat inert. His ghost grounder lay where he'd flung it, its copper rod bent and the rubber glove singed.

His idea turned out to be a disaster, and Vincent had paid the price.

Heart heavy, he wrapped his arm around Vincent's waist for

support. "Come," he said. "Let's get you to the doctor."

"I'm fine, Henry," Vincent said with an air of patient exasperation. "And thanks to Jo, Lizzie is entirely unscathed. Stop moping."

Vincent lay propped up in his bed at the hotel, a white bandage stark against the sienna skin of his forehead. The early light of dawn trickled through the cracks in the shutters and added to the illumination of the gas light on the wall. Henry knew he should have shut off the valve and lit a night candle instead, but after the scene at the cemetery, he found himself wanting as much light as possible.

"If you're fine, it's no thanks to me," he said miserably. The moment when the ghost struck Vincent replayed itself over and over again in his mind. The moment he'd thought Vincent dead, and every possibility of light and happiness drained out of the world.

"It almost worked," Henry added, unable to keep the bitterness from his voice. "We had her weakened. But she was too smart for us."

"That's the problem with intelligent hauntings," Vincent replied. "They're, well, intelligent. Rosanna no doubt received little education as a simple village girl, but she must have been formidably clever. Although not clever enough to avoid falling in love with the wrong man."

"Yes, well, intelligence has nothing to do with love," Henry said.

Was it his imagination, or did Vincent flinch? He lifted his head, but Vincent's expression seemed serene. Imagination, then.

With Ortensi's help, Henry had managed to get Vincent to the doctor, who opened the door rather fearfully at their knock. Fortunately, the man probed Vincent's head carefully, proclaimed his skull in one piece, and recommended rest, so long as someone watched over him. Henry had spent the night at Vincent's bedside, waking him periodically to make certain his condition hadn't worsened. Mostly he sat and thought about how close he'd come to losing Vincent. About how badly he wanted to keep Vincent safe and happy.

About how much Vincent meant to him, with his ridiculous innuendos, and colorful coats, and tender smiles.

"You did your best," Vincent said, reaching out to grasp Henry's hand. "You couldn't have known she'd be able to heat the grounder. Or the wire of the fence." He started to shake his head, then stopped with a grunt of pain. "I certainly didn't think of it. The power she has, to do such a thing…she's very angry. Angry enough to defy three mediums in order to cling to this world. I'm not certain how we're to stop her."

Should he say it? "I have an idea. Not to say my last suggestion was any good."

"You said yourself it almost worked." Vincent frowned uncertainly. "Henry…is everything all right? You seem sad."

Henry couldn't meet Vincent's dark eyes. Vincent had been injured, and Lizzie nearly so. The ghost might have killed them both, under slightly different circumstances. He owed Vincent—owed them all—the truth. He was a failure. The Psychical Society had been right, and he was more than a failure. He was a menace, a danger to them all.

But what if he told the truth now, and Vincent dismissed his idea out of hand?

"I'm only tired," he said. "Just know I appreciate your friendship. The trust you've shown in me. Even if I haven't deserved it."

Vincent's look became even more puzzled. "You do deserve it, Henry," he said. He wrapped his fingers in Henry's, tugging him toward the bed. "Of course I believe in you. You're a brilliant inventor."

Henry pulled free and rose from his chair. "I imagine the others are awake, assuming they slept at all. I should shave. We'll talk more over breakfast, if you're up to it."

He shut the door before Vincent could call him back. Hastening to his own room, he went to the washstand and splashed tepid water on his face. The mirror showed him a haggard face, the line of his jaw darkened with stubble.

He shaved, then changed his cuffs and collar. Anything else felt beyond him at the moment. By the time he arrived back downstairs, everyone else, including Vincent, already awaited him.

"How are you feeling this morning, Lizzie?" Henry enquired as he took his seat.

She held her coffee cup as though it were a lifeline. "The dress is a loss, but I'm quite unharmed, thanks to Jo."

Jo ducked her head. "It wasn't anything," she mumbled at the floor. "I'm glad you and Vincent are all right."

Vincent had removed the doctor's bandage, but his movements were stiff as he reached for the sugar. No doubt the impact with the tree had bruised his entire back. "I told the others you have a suggestion for us, Henry."

Henry took a deep breath. He didn't dare look at Ortensi, at the skepticism he knew he'd—rightfully—see on the medium's face. Rather, he kept his gaze fixed on Vincent.

"I have a way of getting rid of Rosanna," he said. "Or at least, of keeping her from haunting the town any more."

"Another one?" Ortensi asked. "Really, Mr. Strauss, I think we've seen the value of your equipment."

"That isn't fair," Jo protested. At the same time, Vincent said, "We almost succeeded, Sylvester."

Henry huddled deeper into himself. Ortensi was right. "This has nothing to do with my machines," he said quietly. "I propose we give her what she wants."

Lizzie frowned at him. "Give her what she wants?"

"Zadock's bones."

"You want to what?" Vincent asked.

Henry didn't meet his eyes, only stared miserably at his hands. Had the setback of last night truly crushed his spirit so? "I propose we dig up Zadock's remains and reinter them in the old graveyard. Where they originally lay."

"You must be joking!" Vincent stared at Henry. "Rosanna murdered the man in a jealous rage!"

"As Mr. Strauss pointed out when I first told you the legend, we don't know for certain," Sylvester said.

Henry looked up in surprise. "You agree with me?"

"Just because the townspeople believed her a witch doesn't mean she really was one." Sylvester spread his hands apart. "If she was indeed behind the haunting, she would have had to command a very powerful spirit."

"Which would take a necromantic talisman, correct?" Henry asked.

Vincent gripped his coffee cup tightly. The one thing Dunne drilled into them both, again and again, was that their talents were meant to help, not to hurt. Compassion for the dead and the living must be their watchword, always. In light of that, necromancy was surely an abomination, a twisting of their gift into something corrupt and foul.

"If Rosanna killed him using necromancy…the spirit probably possessed Mary." Vincent's gorge rose, and he was glad he hadn't eaten any breakfast. Did Mary awake to find her hands locked around her husband's throat? Or had the spirit been merciful enough to take her while she slept, and she never knew what she had done?

He could still remember the crack as something delicate gave way in Dunne's neck.

"Rosanna was either an innocent or an abomination." Invisible hands seemed locked around his own throat, but Vincent forced out the words. "If the latter, we *can't* give Zadock's bones to his murderer. It would be foul."

"There's nothing to suggest his spirit is anywhere save for the otherworld," Sylvester pointed out gently.

"That's my biggest concern," Henry said. He still seemed taken aback at Sylvester's agreement. "Is his spirit still, ah, attached to his remains? Would he care, after all this time, where his bones lay?"

Vincent's forced his grip to relax before he shattered the coffee cup in his hand. "Does it matter?"

"Vincent." Sylvester's voice was understanding, and grief showed in his hazel eyes. "I know this is difficult for you, but you must think rationally. If Zadock is truly at rest, nothing we do with his bones will change it."

"But—"

"Our charge is the living as well as the dead." Sylvester reached across the table and touched the back of Vincent's hand with his fingers. "Rosanna has already murdered one man. If we hadn't weakened her last night, we might have become her next victims. And what about tonight? And the night after? She is being drawn into a town filled with innocent people. If moving Zadock's bones will confine her to the forest and keep the living of Devil's Walk safe from her depredations, then that is what we must do. Once she's safely ensconced back in the woods, we can consider our next move with a bit more leisure."

Vincent willed his hands to relax beneath Sylvester's light touch. Sylvester was correct on all points, and yet it still seemed wrong somehow. "You're right," he said at last. "I won't pretend to like it, but I have no rational argument against it. Lives are in the balance."

"Lizzie?" Sylvester asked.

She didn't say anything for a long moment. Finally she gave a single, sharp nod. "Agreed."

"So we mean to do it?" Henry said.

"Yes." Sylvester pushed his chair back from the table. "I'll get permission from Mr. Emberey and the mayor, to prevent any misunderstandings."

"A good idea," Henry stood as well. "Come along, Jo. Let's...let's see if we can repair the damage to the phantom fence."

They left. Lizzie turned to Vincent. "What's wrong with Henry?"

"He blames himself for letting Rosanna escape," Vincent said.

She finished her coffee in a single gulp. "That's foolish. And Henry has been acting a bit strange since we arrived. Even for him."

So he wasn't the only one to have noticed. A part of him had hoped it was his own paranoia, his fear the Psychical Society might have given Henry cause to rethink their association. "I tried to speak with him this morning, but he dismissed me."

"Try harder." Lizzie rose to her feet. "This situation is too uncertain. We all need to be focused on the job."

She left. Vincent drank the rest of his coffee in silence, then went to find Henry.

Henry was in the midst of repairing the damaged equipment when he became aware of Vincent standing in the door. Blinking owlishly, he peered up from where he sat on the floor of his tiny room. Vincent leaned against the doorframe, his dark eyes uncharacteristically serious. Had he changed his mind and come to condemn Henry's plan?

"Jo," Vincent said quietly, "would you be so good as to get some coffee for Henry and me?"

"Jo is helping me work," Henry said, even though the request was clearly one for privacy rather than coffee. After his failure last night, he wasn't certain he had the energy to keep up a pretense in front of Vincent.

"It's no trouble." Jo, the traitor, slid off the edge of the bed, where she'd been splicing the wires of the phantom fence back together. "It might take a while, if the kitchen doesn't have any ready."

She left in a whisper of skirts. Henry returned his attention to the ghost grounder. The copper rod sagged sadly in his hand, its shape distorted out of true by the heat Rosanna had summoned.

"I'm not used to seeing your rod this wilted," Vincent remarked, stepping into the room.

"Very funny." At least the ghost grounder should still work, bent or not. Henry set it aside and took a deep breath. "I know you disagree with my suggestion."

"No." Vincent shook his head, then winced at the movement. "I'm uneasy, yes. But Sylvester thinks the idea a good one, given our options."

It shouldn't have hurt, that Vincent would take Ortensi's opinion as more valid than Henry's. Why wouldn't he, given how wrong things had gone last night? "I'm glad the Great Ortensi thought an idea of mine might actually have some merit."

Vincent's thick brows snapped together. "You aren't being fair. Sylvester has been a medium for a long time. He's seen it all. So, yes, I do trust his experience in this matter. I trust it over my own." His expression softened, grew more concerned than angry. "Henry..."

"Jo will be back soon."

Vincent's mouth pressed into a narrower line, but he nodded. "Of course." Stepping closer, he crouched down beside Henry. His warm hand rested on Henry's shoulder, the soft brush of his fingertips against the bare skin at the nape of Henry's neck equal parts comforting and arousing. "Just know if something troubles you, anything at all, you can speak of it to me." His grip tightened. "Whatever it might be."

If only it were true. But Vincent wouldn't understand, no matter what he thought. Henry had spent half his life railing against frauds, and now he was one himself. Vincent would be furious, and rightly so. It would be the end of everything between them. No more comforting touches or gentle smiles. No more waking in the night to feel Vincent's lean arms around him. No more sleepy kisses when he rose for the day, leaving Vincent to snore away the hours until noon.

Each thought was like a tiny razor embedded on the inside of Henry's ribs, slicing into his heart with every beat. How had he been so stupid as to get himself into this mess? If only he'd told the truth the night at the saloon.

If only he hadn't lost his heart so thoroughly in the first place, none of it would have mattered. Not Vincent's opinion of him, or Christopher Maillard's knowing smirks, or any of it. How did he ever imagine he might hold onto someone like Vincent Night, who could have any man he wanted? Cleverness was the only thing Henry had to recommend him; not looks, or an exciting personality, or any of the other things a lover would want.

It had been doomed from the start.

"Vincent?" Ortensi's voice drifted from the end of the hall. "Mr. Strauss? I've secured permission for us to proceed."

"We should go," Henry said. He rose and offered Vincent a hand up.

"Thank you," Vincent said, with another wince. "You should see my back. The bruises make a lovely pattern. I'm thinking about having them copied to wallpaper." He offered Henry a tentative smile. "Perhaps you can help me put salve on them later?"

It might be his last chance for such intimate contact. "I'd love to." His hand lingered on Vincent's, their fingers curling together. "But for now, we should probably go dig up poor Zadock."

CHAPTER 11

VINCENT WATCHED Henry climb out of the hole and wipe the sweat from his brow. Bending over and resting his hands on his knees, Henry gasped, "I think we can remove the coffin now."

Rather than conscript any of the workmen lounging in front of the saloon, they'd decided to undertake the task themselves. It didn't seem likely Rosanna—or, heaven forbid, Zadock—would be able to exert much influence during the daylight hours. Still, Rosanna stalked both Henry and Norris in Devil's Walk Woods during the day. Better safe than sorry.

The old trees cast soothing shadows over the graves, blocking out most of the hot July sun. Emberey, Lizzie, and Jo all stood in the shade, watching while Vincent, Sylvester, and Henry took turns digging. Vincent's shoulders were soon afire, adding to the ache of the bruises discoloring his back. He tried to avoid physical labor whenever possible —and with good reason, given the blisters now decorating his hands and the dirt on his clothing.

Thankfully, the mass reinterment meant the workers buried the coffins just far enough below ground to ensure protection from scavenger or flood. If they'd had to dig through six feet of dirt, Vincent didn't think they would have uncovered the coffin before nightfall. Tomorrow.

Henry sat on the edge of the hole and removed his spectacles.

Taking out a handkerchief, he set about cleaning the glass lenses. "I take it none of you have sensed anything untoward?"

Vincent shook his head. With every shovelful of earth, he'd waited for some foreign flavor to invade his mouth. Dirt or blood, rot or dank water. Ashes and overdone pork. But he tasted nothing but fading coffee and the cinnamon cachous he ate out of habit more than anything else.

"Not a tingle," Sylvester said. "But I would like to make certain."

Henry frowned. "Make certain?"

"Let's get the coffin up first."

Henry and Vincent had already slid ropes around it; now, along with Sylvester, they hauled it free of its very temporary resting place. The moldering wood groaned and creaked, but didn't break. As no doubt befit his position as one of the leading citizens in the old town, Zadock's coffin had been constructed of sturdy materials.

Once it lay to the side of the hole, Sylvester pressed a hand to the small of his back. "Well. Almost done. All we need is a pry bar."

Henry, Jo, and Emberey all looked alarmed. "A pry bar?" Emberey asked.

"We have enough troubles with Rosanna," Sylvester said tiredly. "I've no wish to have Zadock haunting us as well. So, yes, a pry bar."

A cart waited outside the graveyard, ready to transport the coffin back to its original resting place in the old town. A quick word to the man driving it produced a pry bar in short order.

"If the rest of you would step outside the churchyard and close the iron gate, I'd be grateful," Sylvester said.

Henry frowned. "Why?"

"I mean to open the coffin and disturb the remains," Sylvester replied. "We've received no hint Zadock's spirit yet lingers in this world, or cares at all about his earthly body. But I don't intend to leave this to chance. Handling his bones should tell us definitively one way or the other."

"I'll stay and help," Vincent said.

Sylvester offered him a tired smile. "I appreciate the offer, but I only sent everyone else away as a precaution. I don't truly think there will be any danger."

"Please, Sylvester, let one of us stay," Lizzie said. "Just in case."

For a long moment, Sylvester gazed at them both. Concern showed in his hazel eyes, reminding Vincent irresistibly of Dunne, who always worried for the apprentices in his care.

But Dunne was dead, and Vincent no longer an apprentice. "You know we're right."

"Of course." Sylvester's concern eased into a wry smile. "You're absolutely correct. Vincent, stay with me."

"Perhaps I should remain as well?" Henry offered.

Sylvester's smile slipped away. "Thank you for the offer, Mr. Strauss. But this is a case where your instruments aren't called for. I'm at a loss to think what you might do should I prove wrong and danger come upon us."

Henry's shoulders slumped, and to Vincent's surprise, he didn't argue. "I...yes. Of course."

Soon Vincent and Sylvester were alone with the unearthed coffin. "Allow me," Vincent said, reaching for the pry bar. He might be sore and bruised, but Sylvester had a good three decades on him.

Thankfully, the nails pulled free of the aged wood with ease. Vincent dragged the lid aside and stared down at the pitiful remains within.

Whatever Zadock's appearance in life, death had left him nothing more than a jumble of rag and bone. The previous disinterment had jolted the remains: the skull had rolled free, vertebrae mingled with finger bones, and ribs with toes. The ivory arch of the pelvis showed through rotting cloth, whatever color it might have been dyed black by the decaying body it covered.

The stench of death had long dissipated, leaving behind only the scent of rich earth. Vincent swished his tongue against his teeth, then opened his mouth and took a deep breath.

"Nothing," he reported.

Sylvester nodded. "Let's hope it stays that way."

Sylvester crouched beside the coffin and began to handle the bones —the skull, a femur. He brushed aside cloth, inspecting a wedding ring, the rusted lump of a belt buckle, and a series of brass buttons.

Still nothing.

Sylvester investigated the remains thoroughly. At length, he sat back on his heels. A pensive look crossed his face.

"Is something wrong?" Vincent asked. "Did you feel some trace of his spirit?"

"What? No." Sylvester shook his head, as if coming back to himself. Flexing his fingers, he said, "I felt nothing, in terms of emotion or physical sensation. Let's get him to the forest, before the sun can go down."

"What a charming way to spend an afternoon," Vincent said, shoving the coffin lid back into place. "I should have thought to bring a picnic."

Vincent sat on the edge of his bed and wondered tiredly if he could remove his clothing without too much pain and effort, of if he should just collapse onto the blankets and fall asleep fully dressed.

His head ached, and his back and arms ached even worse. He'd washed the worst of the dust and dirt from his face and hands, but the prospect of struggling out of his coat, let alone bending over to untie his shoes, seemed far too daunting to face.

The sun went down just as they left the woods behind. There'd been no incidents on the way to the old town, nor back from it. Nothing but a sense of watchfulness as they reburied Zadock's coffin in one of the empty holes beside the church. No taste of ashes on his tongue; no tingle in Sylvester's fingertips.

At least tonight the townsfolk would sleep peacefully, for the first time in days. The ghost still needed to be dealt with, of course, so the steel mill could be built without spectral interference. But for now she'd remain in the woods, content with her lover's bones.

There came a soft knock on the door. "Come in," he said automatically.

Henry stuck his head inside, the dark honey of his hair damp from washing. The summer sun had tinged his forehead and cheeks pink, and brought out a spray of freckles across his nose. Unlike their first night here, when they'd had adjacent rooms, he remained fully dressed. "May I come in?"

"Please." Vincent started to make a welcoming gesture, but was brought up short when his back spasmed.

Henry noticed, of course. "How are you feeling?" he asked as he shut the door behind him.

"As though a ghost threw me into a tree, before I spent the day doing unfamiliar physical labor in the hot sun."

"I can't imagine why," Henry said dryly, before casting a nervous glance at the wall, having forgotten to keep his voice down.

Vincent took his meaning. "Don't worry. Thanks to the ghost, the hotel is rather empty, other than our group. There's no one to either side of me. I wouldn't suggest you spend the entire night, but we can converse freely."

Henry crossed the room. "In that case, tell me what I can do for you."

Vincent wagged a suggestive brow. Henry snorted. "What *else* I can do for you."

"Honestly, I'm so tired I've just been sitting here trying to work up the energy to get out of my clothes," Vincent confessed.

"Then allow me to help."

Henry gently peeled off Vincent's coat, batting away his hands when Vincent reached for the buttons on his vest. Henry undid each button and those of the shirt beneath, then knelt and removed Vincent's shoes.

Soon Vincent's skin was exposed to the relatively cool night air wafting through the open window. "Lie on your stomach," Henry instructed, going to the washstand.

Henry let out a sympathetic hiss when he saw Vincent's back. "My poor Vincent. You must be in pain."

Vincent smiled against the pillow. *My poor Vincent. My Vincent.* Maybe not forever, but for now…for tonight…Henry wanted him.

The soft touch of a damp cloth swiped across his shoulder. "Let me know if I hurt you," Henry said.

"I will," Vincent lied. But there was no pain in this. Just tenderness. The gentle kiss of the washcloth, cleaning away sweat and grime. And Henry's kisses, dotted one on each shoulder, in the center of Vincent's spine, right at the cleft of his buttocks. Little kisses, sweet rather than passionate.

"Turn over."

Vincent's cock bobbed lazily, semi-erect from his lover's touch. Henry had shed his own coat and vest, and rolled up his sleeves. "You must be sore yourself," Vincent said. "You're no more used to digging holes than I. And you took two turns while uncovering Zadock, and I only one."

"True, but I'm not the one with a cracked head and a bruised back."

"My head isn't cracked," Vincent mumbled. "The doctor said so."

The cloth traced patterns across Vincent's chest. "That's because he'd never met you."

Vincent pretended shock. "I'm wounded, sir! Wounded to the—oh!"

Henry's mouth closed around his prick. His thoughts scattered as it seemed all the blood in his body rushed to bring his cock to full attention. "Henry…"

A soft whimper escaped him when Henry let his cock slip free. "Shh," Henry said. "Let me tend to you. Unless you wish me to stop?"

"No, of course not. I'll return the favor, naturally."

Henry's hand rested on Vincent's hip. "You're exhausted, and I won't ask it of you. Just let me do this for you, Vincent. Please."

Vincent could count on one hand the number of people who'd cared enough about him to do anything for him without wanting something in return. The girl—sister? mother?—who featured in his earliest memories. Dunne. Lizzie. Sylvester.

Men in alleys wanted pleasure in exchange for money. Or for nothing, if they were cruel enough with their fists. Lovers gave pleasure in return for pleasure of their own. A transaction, where everyone involved knew where they stood.

Being with Henry was like walking on quicksand. Henry did things for other people without always thinking of himself. There was no transaction, no checking of the balance sheets to see who owed what.

A moan escaped Vincent. Henry's mouth was warm and wet, his tongue playing along the underside of his shaft, the lightest nip of teeth at the very tip of Vincent's cock, before plunging back down again. And oh God, Vincent *wanted* this—not just the sex, not even mainly the sex, but the kindness, and the laughter, and Henry's oh-so-clever mind. His enthusiasm and his confidence, both of which had been so strangely lacking over the last few days.

"Henry," he whispered—no, pleaded, desperate. *I'm yours; I want to be yours,* but he locked the words behind his teeth, because he had no right to demand such things. Not now, not when Henry stood right on the cusp of fame...

His next cry was wordless, a rush of ecstasy, thought obliterated in a moment where he could do nothing but cling to the bed sheets while Henry moaned around his cock.

With a sigh, Henry drew back, licking his lips. "I take it you were satisfied with my performance?"

Vincent flung out an arm, feeling nearly boneless. "More than. Are you certain...?"

Henry pressed a kiss against eyelids that had somehow slipped closed. "You're drifting off in front of me. Just scoot over. I want to hold you for a while, before I have to leave."

Vincent obeyed. "Can't wait until we get back to Baltimore," he mumbled against the pillow.

The mattress gave as Henry crawled in beside Vincent. He'd stripped, and tucked his erection between his thighs, presumably to avoid poking Vincent unduly. "Why?"

"So I can wake up beside you."

Henry was silent, and for an awful moment Vincent began to think he'd said something wrong. Then Henry's lips pressed against the back of his shoulder. "Agreed."

Henry lingered for more hours than prudence dictated, and it neared midnight when he pulled on his trousers and buttoned his vest. Vincent lay sleeping in the bed, the soft glow of the night candle burnishing his skin. Henry's heart ached at the sight, as if some ghostly hand slipped inside his chest and squeezed hard.

They'd half finished their duty here. With Rosanna back in the woods with her lover's bones, bereft of the energy of the townsfolk's fears, a medium like Ortensi would surely be able to send her to the otherworld. Then they'd go home to Baltimore. And Henry would no longer be able to put off his confession.

Tonight might have been their last night together. If not, certainly it must number one of the last.

Ignoring the burning behind his eyelids, Henry bent to retrieve his shoes. He'd put them on once in the hall, to keep from waking Vincent. His own sore muscles gave a twinge when he stood up again.

As he turned to the door, the scent of smoke drifting through the open window caught his attention. Who on earth would have a fire going at this time of night, in this heat?

The Franklin bells began to ring.

Vincent's dark eyes shot open, and a gasp escaped him. "Rosanna. She's here."

"She can't be," Henry protested. "We gave her what she wanted. There's nothing left to tie her to the town."

Vincent rolled out of bed, yanking his drawers up over narrow hips. "Something must have gone wrong. She's nearby. Damn it!"

Fear iced Henry's veins. "The fire. You don't think...?"

"I think we'd better hurry," Vincent replied grimly. Trousers in place, his slender fingers flew over the buttons of his shirt. Abandoning vest and coat alike, he pushed past Henry. "Come on!"

They ran through the hall and down the stairs. "Fire!" Vincent shouted. "In the town!"

Muffled cries of alarm and inquiry followed them, but they didn't slow. Outside, the smell of burning grew even stronger, and a column of smoke rose against the sky, blotting out the stars. Shouts rang through the night, some calling for a bucket brigade. Others though...cries of "devil" and "witchery" and "the ghost has come for us" sent sparks of panic into the air.

The burning building stood one row back from the main street. As they rounded the corner, Henry let out a shocked oath. Despite the tightly packed houses, at the moment only a single structure burned, the fire confined to its blackening beams.

As for the flames themselves...they burned not with a wholesome red and yellow, but rather the sickly blue of the grave.

Three children stood in the street in front of the house, screaming and clinging to each other in panic. "Is there anyone still inside?" Henry called.

"Mama! Da!" shrieked the youngest.

Oh God. Henry turned to the conflagration with a sinking heart. Holding up one arm as if to shield himself, he started forward. A wave of heat struck him, so intense it seemed to suck the moisture from his very lungs. Smoke billowed from the burning house, turning the night even darker. There came the crack and groan of weakening beams...

"Henry, no!" Vincent's hand seized his left shoulder. A sharp point of pain flared through the old wound. "No one could survive in there!"

The wails of the children dinned in Henry's ears, almost drowned beneath the hungry roar of the flames. "The ghost did this!" he shouted, trying to pull free from Vincent's grasp. "We were supposed to get rid of her, and she came back, and she did this! This is our fault!"

No. It was Henry's fault. He'd suggested reburying the bones. The idea had failed, just as his trap in the cemetery failed.

And now people were dead. Because of him.

Ortensi let out a pained cry behind them. "Sylvester!" Vincent cried, letting go of Henry. The other medium crouched in the road, not far from the huddled children, his hands pressed to his temples.

"She's furious," Ortensi groaned. "God! Stop, please!"

Vincent caught Ortensi by the elbows. "Focus, Sylvester. Deep breaths. Center yourself. You aren't her; her pain isn't yours."

"What can we do?" Henry demanded. He'd run out here with nothing—no ghost grounder, not even a handful of salt. A sense of helplessness seized him, and he turned again to the roaring flames.

Their eerie blue light seemed to have frightened away any hope of a bucket brigade. Even as he watched, there came another groan, followed by a roar as the roof and upper floor collapsed. Sparks flew madly into the air—but they didn't spread to the houses around them. As if some force held them in check still.

Something moved in the flames.

For a mad instant, he thought it might be one of the missing parents, even though nothing living could possibly have survived such heat. The flames coalesced into hair, flushing orange-red amidst the blue. The blank white eyes of the ghost stared at him, into him, as if mining the very depths of his soul.

"Vincent," he whispered. "R-run." But his own feet stuck to the earth as she advanced on him.

"Bring him back," she snarled in a voice like dry leaves catching fire. *"Bring him back; BRING HIM BACK; BRING HIM BACK!"*

"Henry!" Vincent seized him, dragging Henry to the ground. A burst of heat rolled over them, and terrified screams filled the night.

"She's gone," Vincent said a moment later. He sat back on his heels. Henry raised his head. The other townsfolk who came to help either huddled in terror, or else fled, all hope of a bucket brigade abandoned. At the moment, he couldn't blame them.

"Vincent," he whispered, and pointed at the house across the way. "Look."

Before departing, Rosanna had left a final message. Burned into the wooden siding of the house was a single word.

TOMORROW.

CHAPTER 12

"**YOU WILL** give me a full accounting of this disaster," Emberey said the next morning. A mixture of sleeplessness and anger shadowed his eyes, and he glowered at them over the breakfast table. "You said the ghost would be pacified by moving Zadock's body. You assured me her activities would be confined to the woods. You claimed she'd be weakened without the fear of the townsfolk to draw upon! And instead, one of my foremen is dead and the entire town is in a panic!"

Henry stared at the untouched eggs on his plate, slowly turning rubbery as they cooled. He had no appetite, couldn't even imagine ever being hungry again. At least only the one house had burned—so far.

"Was it a warning?" he wondered aloud. "Will she return tonight and burn the rest of us?"

Vincent's hand found his beneath the shield of the tablecloth. "Let Sylvester speak," he said quietly.

"I understand you're upset, Mr. Emberey," Ortensi said. His voice sounded hoarse, from either lack of sleep or from breathing in too much smoke. Perhaps both. "I can only say we truly believed Rosanna to be searching for the bones of her lover. That by returning him, we would curtail the worst aspects of the haunting and buy ourselves the chance to act."

"Well clearly you were wrong," Emberey snapped. "I'm paying you a great deal of money to remove this ghost, and what have you accomplished? Nothing! Norris is dead, and now Mr. and Mrs. Brooks have perished as well. My workers are fleeing the town—those who can't afford train tickets are setting off on foot, with nothing save the clothes on their backs. I cannot build a mill under these conditions, Mr. Ortensi!"

"No, sir," Ortensi agreed. His mouth pressed into a flat line, and Henry thought resentment flickered in his eyes, there and gone again. "I can only say the supernatural isn't always straightforward. We have done everything in our power to end this, and will continue to do so."

Henry closed his eyes, then opened them again. Nausea turned his stomach, his eyes aching from lack of sleep. "She only burned one house." He focused on the memory, the heat and flames, the sparks so oddly confined. "Why? And why that one?"

Lizzie stirred for the first time. She and Jo had arrived at the blaze too late to do anything but help Ortensi back to the hotel and find a cool cloth to ease his subsequent headache. "Who lived in the house?"

"Mr. and Mrs. Walter Brooks," Emberey said. "And their three children."

"Brooks." Vincent sat back and looked at Ortensi. "We…well, not met him, exactly. He was the foreman Mr. Emberey demoted."

Ortensi's eyes widened slightly. "You're right."

"Yes, yes." Emberey waved an impatient hand. "What does it matter?"

"Norris. Brooks. Rosanna killed them both." Ortensi frowned. "There must be a connection!"

"It seems likely," Henry offered. "And their children were staying elsewhere?" Their sobs and cries still seemed to ring in his ears.

To his surprise, Jo shook her head. "No. After we got there, while Lizzie helped Mr. Ortensi, I asked the girls what I could do. They told me what happened."

Henry straightened. "What did they say?"

She glanced between him and Emberey. "They said they slept in the downstairs room, just like always. Their mother and father were upstairs in the bedroom. They woke up to find a lady standing over them. She yelled at them to get out." Jo bit her lip. "As soon as they set foot outside, the whole house caught on fire. As if it was just waiting for them to leave."

"The legend says the ghost spared the children when the original Whispering Falls burned," Ortensi murmured. "Apparently she's still repeating the pattern."

"Which gets us precisely nowhere." Emberey scowled. "What does it matter if the ghost has a woman's soft heart for children, if she burns down the town and kills the rest of us?"

Henry bit back a protest. He could only hope Emberey didn't have any offspring of his own. "We should speak to them," he said instead. "I…I know I've no right to make any suggestions, but perhaps they can shed some light as to why the ghost took their parents?"

"A good point," Ortensi said, rather unexpectedly. "Perhaps you and I can question them, Mr. Strauss."

Why this sudden apparent peace offering, Henry had no idea. "Of course."

"And while you're engaged," Lizzie said, "I'll pursue another avenue of inquiry."

A frown creased Vincent's handsome face. "Lizzie?"

She folded her hands on the table in front of her. "Our attempts at guessing what the ghost wants have come to nothing. Therefore, I intend to ask her directly."

"An automatic writing session?" Henry asked. At the same moment, Vincent exclaimed, "You can't be serious!"

"Yes, and I'm very serious." Her expression remained smooth, unruffled. Admitting no doubt.

"No." Ortensi leaned across the table and fixed Lizzie with his gaze. "I forbid it."

"Sylvester—"

"No," he repeated. "At least, not yet. Let Mr. Strauss and I discover what we can in a less hazardous fashion. If we fail, we'll discuss other options. But I won't have you risk this unless there is no other choice."

Lizzie's mouth tightened. "I know you're concerned, Sylvester, but you saw what the ghost wrote. 'Tomorrow.' We don't know exactly what she meant, but finding out will likely result in more deaths."

He reached over the table and took her hand. "Trust me, Lizzie. Please."

For a moment, Henry thought she'd argue. Then she let out a long sigh. "Very well, Sylvester. If you insist."

Emberey rose to his feet. "If you've settled on your work, get to it," he ordered. "This has gone on long enough. You will remove this ghost, or I'll find someone who can."

The streets of Devil's Walk were busier than Henry had yet seen. Several families piled furniture, clothing, and other belongings into carts.

Groups of men hurried in the direction of the train station, while a few others pushed handcarts along the road heading out of town.

Many of them glared at Henry and Ortensi. "You were supposed to keep us safe!" a woman shouted. Henry flinched, but Ortensi kept walking, his head up and his back straight, until they reached the site of last night's fire.

The scent of wood smoke still lingered in the air while a group of men worked to clear away the burned wreckage. Whatever didn't seem of use was piled into a cart, while other items appeared to be set aside for sorting. Given the intensity of the flames, little of the last category remained.

They stopped work when Henry and Ortensi approached. The man in charge seemed to recognize them; his eyes narrowed into a scowl. "What do you want?" he asked Ortensi. "Haven't you already done enough?"

"Not by half," one of the others muttered. "They ain't stopped the ghost. Maybe they've made her angrier."

An ugly sound of agreement rumbled through the group at the final suggestion. Henry's heartbeat quickened as he glanced from unfriendly face to unfriendly face. These men were rough, work-hardened, with dirt beneath their fingernails and skin weathered from the sun. He was suddenly, painfully aware of the picture he must present to them, with his clean-but-shabby suit and skin gone pale from long hours in his shop. Certainly he lacked their musculature. If they decided he and Ortensi were easy prey, just soft outsiders whose failure made them ideal scapegoats, things might turn ugly.

Ortensi seemed undisturbed, however. His gold rings flashed as he spread his hands apart. "It's true—we believed we had defeated the enemy." His voice boomed like an orator's, conveying a mixture of grief and determination. "But she has proved far more resilient than expected, and has taken her revenge against a good man. We will bring her to justice, gentlemen—this I swear. But we must discover why she made Mr. Brooks her target."

There came a shuffling and muttering. "What, you think she was after Walt for some reason?" someone asked.

Henry gestured to the ruins. "The fire claimed only this house, when it could have—*should* have, by the laws of nature—spread to those beside it."

"Does anyone know why the ghost might have focused on Mr. Brooks?" Ortensi asked. "Did he do anything odd at the work site in the woods, perhaps? Take anything from it?"

There came a general shaking of heads. "You can ask his daughters, though," one said, and pointed down the street. "They're staying with their uncle and aunt. Third to last house on the left."

"Thank you, gentlemen." Ortensi gave a little bow, then turned and started in the direction indicated. Henry hurried after him.

"Well done," Henry said, once they were out of earshot. "For a moment, I feared they intended to give us a beating instead of information."

"I've long experience working crowds," Ortensi said with a wave of his hand. His expression sharpened slightly, and he glanced at Henry. "May I speak frankly, Mr. Strauss?"

The words put Henry on edge. This must be why Ortensi chose him instead of Vincent for this task. "Of course."

"You seem somewhat fond of Vincent."

Somewhat fond? What the devil did Ortensi mean? Did he guess their relationship, or did he merely think them business partners? "I am," he said guardedly. "I believe we work rather well together."

"A point on which I'm afraid I don't agree."

Henry came to a shocked halt. "Pardon me?"

Ortensi stopped as well, a look of sympathy on his face. "Forgive my bluntness, Mr. Strauss. I'm certain your inventions have merit— Vincent spoke to me of your recent triumph before the Psychical Society."

All the moisture seemed to have evaporated from Henry's mouth. "D-Did he?"

"But Vincent is a medium, not a tinkerer such as yourself," Ortensi went on. "And I fear, due to your differences, you can't truly appreciate the extent of his gifts. He can do better than a tiny shop in Baltimore."

Henry's heart sank. "I...I'm sure he could."

"I'm glad you agree. You'll understand, then, when I say I mean to ask him to accompany me to Europe."

A cry of objection half-escaped Henry, before he closed his throat around it. The idea of Vincent leaving, of sailing off to another continent, forever out of Henry's reach, felt like a live animal clawing its way out of his chest.

Losing Vincent was inevitable. He had no choice but to accept the idea. But he hadn't expected the reality to come like this. Not yet.

"I..." he said, but no other words would come.

Ortensi gave him a look tinged with pity. "You see it's for the best, don't you? Vincent is a great medium, one of the best I've had the privilege of meeting, but his talents are wasted here. In Europe, his heritage will be an advantage. Crowds will flock to see the genuine Indian medicine man, come all the way from the Americas."

"Vincent isn't a—a sideshow attraction," Henry snapped.

"Nor do I mean for him to be one. But his skin will open doors to him that would remain closed here." Ortensi shook his head. "If you are his friend, you must know I speak truly."

"I see." The clawing thing in his chest had escaped, leaving him hollow. A part of Henry wanted to argue, to point out Vincent might not agree to leave with Ortensi.

And Henry would have…if only he had something to offer Vincent in return. Something more than an empty promise that someday, somehow, they might find themselves performing before the noble families of Europe.

Ortensi could offer such fame now. Henry had nothing but a handful of lies and a workshop filled with devices proved largely worthless.

"I'm glad you understand." Ortensi's hand came to rest on Henry's shoulder, a heavy weight he didn't want to bear. "I worried Vincent might refuse me out of loyalty, which is why I chose to speak to you now."

"Yes, I…yes." Words chased each other through Henry's mind, but they were all meaningless. "Vincent is free to accompany you. I have no…no claim on him."

Ortensi's fingers tightened, then he removed his hand. "Good. But for now, let's see to our work."

The man who opened the door at Ortensi's knock greeted them with a glower. His scowl remained fixed while Ortensi explained why they'd come. When the medium finished, the man spat, barely missing Henry's shoes.

"You were supposed to get rid of the ghost," he growled. "Instead, I've got a dead brother and three more mouths to feed. What about my own children, huh? What about them? Are they supposed to go hungry so I can feed Walter's brats?"

"I'm very sorry for your loss, Mr. Brooks," Ortensi replied. "But if we're to have any hope of stopping the ghost, we have to find out why she targeted your brother."

Brooks's scowl turned into a look of fear. "Targeted Walt? You mean she was after him?"

"It would seem so."

He glanced over his shoulder. "And she'll come after us next, as we took in the girls?"

"No!" Henry exclaimed. As soon as the words left his mouth, he knew he couldn't make such a statement for certain. But from the look on Brooks's face, the man meant to turn the children out if he thought there existed the slightest chance of danger.

"May we speak to you about your brother?" Ortensi asked. "About the work he did on the mill site?"

Brooks took a step back, as if he might shut the door in their faces. "I don't know nothing about it. Walt put on airs, him being a foreman and all. Too high and mighty for the likes of me. Now he's gone and gotten himself killed by a ghost."

Wonderful. "His daughters, perhaps?" Henry tried. "I don't wish to deepen their grief, but if we might speak to them?"

Brooks shrugged. "Suit yourself."

They followed him into the small home. The three girls worked in the kitchen, alongside another girl and a woman who must be Mrs. Brooks. "These men need to talk to you about your daddy," Brooks said.

Tears welled in the eyes of the younger two. The eldest blinked rapidly, but stepped away from the vegetables she'd been slicing. "I'll do it," she said, giving Ortensi and Henry a little curtsey. "Nellie and Irene can stay here."

Considering the other two were probably too young to question anyway, Henry nodded. "Thank you, Miss Brooks. Perhaps we can speak in the parlor?"

After refusing an offer of food and drink, they settled into the parlor. Miss Brooks sat with her eyes downcast and her hands folded into her apron. She appeared around fourteen—the same age as Jo, when she came to Henry. Leaning forward slightly, so as not to loom above her, he said, "We're very sorry for your loss, Miss Brooks. And please believe me, the last thing I want is to upset you further."

"Not sure as that's possible, sir," she said.

"Of course." He glanced at Ortensi, but the medium seemed content to let Henry continue. Perhaps he thought Henry of some use after all. "Before last night, did anything odd catch your attention? Anything about your father?"

She shook her head. "No."

"Did he seem worried about something, perhaps?" This would be easier if he had a better idea what questions to ask. "Something to do with the steel mill, or the woods, or the ghost?"

"Just that the work stopped, and he wasn't getting paid." She chewed on her lip. "He was angry at Mr. Emberey and at Mr. Ortensi for not doing more. Sorry, sir."

"Quite all right," Ortensi said. "Miss Brooks, I must ask...last night, you told Miss Strauss that a woman woke you from slumber, before the fire began."

Her lower lip began to tremble, and she wrapped her arms around herself. "Y-Yes," she said in a small voice. "We sleep—slept—in the back room downstairs. I woke up, and a lady was standing over us, only...only all burned up!"

The horror in her voice dug into Henry's heart like a rusty hook. "Go on, Miss Brooks. You've been very brave."

"Th-thank you, sir. She was so awful, I wanted to scream, but all the breath seemed frozen in my lungs. The cold was unnatural. She said to get out, and to take my sisters with me. And she said...she said she was sorry."

Ortensi frowned. "Sorry?"

"Yes." She nodded. "I just...I grabbed Irene and Nellie, and we ran. And a minute later, the house was on fire." Tears slid down her face. "I should've woken Mama and Da, I should've..."

"You saved the lives of your sisters," Henry said. He took his handkerchief from his pocket and passed it to the weeping girl. "It was the right decision, no matter how difficult. Never doubt it."

She nodded, probably in too much pain to answer.

Ortensi rose to his feet, and Henry hastily did the same. "Thank you for your time, Miss Brooks. You've been most helpful."

As soon as they were out on the street again, Henry said, "Rosanna saved the children. Just as the legend claimed."

"Hardly something we didn't already know," Ortensi replied.

"Perhaps, but she apologized. Why?"

"For killing their parents?" Ortensi shrugged. "It doesn't matter. The child knew nothing of substance."

None of it sat well with Henry. Why did Rosanna save the children, both when she died and now? Why apologize for making these three into orphans, dependent on their uncle's bare charity?

"She's a spirit of rage," he said aloud.

"Yes," Ortensi replied. "What of it?"

"I don't know. I wonder...Vincent told me the old parish records from Whispering Falls were in the church."

Ortensi eyed him uncertainly. "Yes. Why?"

"Just a feeling. I want to look at them." Henry turned away. "I won't be long. Go back to the hotel without me."

CHAPTER 13

HENRY WALKED quickly to the church, keeping his eyes averted from the graveyard. The hole where they'd exhumed Zadock's bones still gaped open, like a mouth accusing him of failure one more time.

Would Mr. and Mrs. Brooks be laid to rest in the convenient hole, or did they already have a burial plot? And what would happen to their daughters, now at the mercy of a man who didn't want them?

The church door creaked as he opened it. A small group of people clustered on the pews. "Deliver us from evil," an old woman prayed aloud. "Lord, save us from the scourge of the witch! Protect us from this minion of the devil!"

Fitzwilliam claimed God sent the witch to punish the town. Clearly his fellow townsfolk considered Satan to be the responsible party. They cast Henry curious looks as he passed by.

"Just checking something," he said, gesturing vaguely in the direction of the vestry door. "To help us stop the, er, witch."

Either the group trusted him not to misbehave in a church, or didn't care. At any rate, no one moved to stop him.

Vincent had mentioned the condition of the old record book, so it took little effort for Henry to find it on the bottom shelf. Henry took the crumbling book up carefully and laid it on the desk. The pages threatened to fall to pieces when he opened it, and he held his breath as he searched for the last records.

Vincent and Ortensi had dismissed Lizzie's earlier speculation that Rosanna had greater cause for anger than lovesickness over Zadock. But Henry couldn't help but wonder if Lizzie had been right all along. If the clue—Rosanna's consistent sparing of children—hadn't in fact been in front of them the entire time.

The entry appeared not far from the end, just below the record of Zadock and Mary's wedding. *Rosanna Cooper, delivered of a son. Stillborn. No man acknowledges paternity.*

Burial on consecrated ground refused.

Henry stared at the damning words until they swam before his gaze. Surely the child belonged to Zadock.

How must Rosanna have felt, holding her dead infant in her arms, when Zadock refused to acknowledge his son? Or when the church turned its back, judging the child unfit to be laid to rest on consecrated ground because its father married another woman?

She'd been angry. Of course she had. Something so petty as sexual jealousy hadn't motivated her vengeance against Zadock. It had been the deep rage over his betrayal of their child.

Henry closed the book and bent his head back, massaging his neck.

Inscribed on the wall directly in front of him, which had been blank only moments before, were the words: HELP ME.

He stumbled back, casting about frantically. But there came no show of violence, no stench of burned flesh.

"Help you?" The words grated out of his throat, but he tamped down on his fear. "Help you how? Help…oh. Never mind. I understand."

Rosanna didn't want them to bring Zadock's bones back.

The bones she sought belonged to her son.

"This is terrible news," Ortensi said. "We've no idea where her son's bones might lie."

They sat in the small private parlor, arrayed around the table on which the moldering parish records lay. Henry had surreptitiously smuggled them from the church beneath his coat, his body turned to hide his theft from the worshippers. Likely the pastor wouldn't notice, even if he did return before Henry put them back.

"His remains wouldn't be in Devil's Walk, would they?" Jo asked. "If he wasn't buried in the churchyard, I mean."

Ortensi shook his head. "They could be, I'm afraid. In the old days, illegitimate or unbaptized children denied burial in the churchyard were often snuck into the coffins of adults who died around the same time. A small bribe to the undertaker would ensure the tiny body was hidden beneath the larger corpse, with no one else the wiser. Or a desperate parent might take the risk of sneaking into the cemetery and digging into a fresh grave, where the loosened soil from the second burial wouldn't be noticed."

"Abominable," Vincent muttered. "To refuse comfort to a distraught parent, to drive them to such measures…"

"You'll get no argument from me," Ortensi replied. "We can only be thankful such practices have died out. But my point is the child might have been snuck into a coffin, or buried after. We've no idea which, or whose coffin."

"The records," Henry suggested. "Who died around the same time the baby was born?" He pulled the book closer and scanned the entries. "Here is a Mr. Tanner…and a Mrs. Smyth…and a Mr. Martin."

"Damn it," Vincent said. Lizzie shot him a reproving look, and he said, "Excuse my language, ladies. But we don't have time to dig up every possible grave where the baby might have been concealed. Rosanna wrote *tomorrow* on the wall, which I must remind you is now *today*. If she intends to wreak her vengeance, we have only a few hours left to stop her."

"I don't understand why she targeted Mr. Brooks and Mr. Norris, though," Jo said.

Ortensi's chair creaked. "It is a puzzle. Perhaps she believed them involved in his disinterment somehow. If Brooks was the foreman, and Norris…well, I'm not entirely sure. Perhaps he was merely in the wrong place at the wrong time. It hardly matters at this point, however. We must act."

"I agree." Lizzie straightened in her chair, fixing her green eyes on Ortensi. "I understand your concern, Sylvester, but I cannot allow fear for my safety to endanger others. The ghost clearly wishes to communicate through writing. I have the best chance of any of us to successfully channel her. Perhaps we can even reason with her, now that we know what she wants."

Vincent shifted in his chair, every line of his body radiating unhappiness. "Lizzie…" He trailed off.

She held herself regally, like a queen preparing for battle. "I know you're worried for me, Vincent, but we have no choice and you know it."

Ortensi nodded reluctantly. "I fear Elizabeth is correct. But I would suggest we conduct the séance not here, but in the forest."

"What on earth for?" Henry asked, surprised. "Wouldn't that be ten times more dangerous?"

But Lizzie nodded her agreement. "Sylvester's right, Henry. She's a spirit of fire. If she becomes enraged or strikes out at us, at least it won't spread to the rest of Devil's Walk. And if we can keep her attention on us there, perhaps it will dissuade her from carrying out her threat against the townspeople here."

The plan sat uneasily in Henry's gut. Then again, perhaps he was simply being irrational, after the fright Rosanna gave him amidst the trees. "Logical," he admitted. "Very well. Jo and I will pack up what instruments and equipment we can carry, and—"

"I think not, Mr. Strauss," Ortensi said flatly.

Henry stopped, stunned. Beside him, Vincent frowned at Ortensi. "Sylvester?"

Ortensi's expression grew even graver, like a judge about to pronounce a terrible sentence. "I'll admit, looking at the old parish records based on Rosanna's avoidance of harming children was a lucky guess," he said. "But luck only goes so far. Your devices and instruments have failed to impress me. Reliance on them led to injury to Vincent, and might have killed Elizabeth had Miss Strauss not acted quickly."

A lead weight lay in Henry's gut. "I...I know it must seem so..."

"Moreover, I will not have a man I don't trust at my back in such a perilous situation." Ortensi's eyebrows lowered threateningly. "You've been lying about something since the beginning, Mr. Strauss. I suggest you come clean now."

"I..." How did Ortensi know? He cast a frantic glance at Vincent, who frowned at Ortensi.

"Sylvester, we've already discussed this," Vincent said. "I told you, Henry is neither a liar nor a fraud."

The faith in Vincent's statement cut deep. For a moment, Henry wanted nothing more than to let the lie go on. Just a little while longer.

And when Vincent found out what Henry had done? Would it hurt even more, to know Henry sat silent, while Vincent defended him to Ortensi?

"Mr. Ortensi is right," he said.

Silence fell over the little room, even the rustles of ordinary movement gone, as if his words had frozen them all. Henry stared down at his hands, unable to meet Vincent's gaze, or Lizzie's, or even Jo's. "I haven't been...entirely honest about things. Things related to my theories and equipment. To our work."

"Henry?" Jo asked, and a hand seemed to squeeze his lungs at the concern in her voice.

"I lied about my reception from the Psychical Society." He licked dry lips. "Dr. Kelly didn't praise my work. He…condemned it. I'll get no new jobs, no new contacts, from the society. In fact, I've been barred from setting foot amongst them again."

Agonizing silence followed his statement. He felt like a condemned man, waiting for the jury to pronounce their verdict. His palms sweated, and his heart beat too fast. He couldn't look anywhere but at his own fingers.

"Why?" Lizzie demanded. "Why in the world would you lie to us?"

"I…" But what could he say?

"Clearly, Mr. Strauss wished to present himself as something he was not," Ortensi said, a hint of smugness in the words. "To drum up his accomplishments in hopes of praise or money. The usual reasons people commit such fraud."

Henry wanted to argue, but the words wouldn't seem to come. "I'm sorry," he managed. "I know I've disappointed you all, I know it. But, please, give me the chance to make it up to you."

Vincent's chair scraped against the floor. Startled by the sudden movement, Henry looked up. Vincent had already turned from him and started for the door.

And maybe he'd already lost Vincent, but it couldn't end like this. The sight of Vincent walking away drove Henry to his feet. "No," he said, stretching his hand out. "Please, don't leave."

Vincent didn't indicate he'd even heard Henry's ragged plea. His footsteps faded down the hall.

"Well," Ortensi said. "Now that this bit of business has finally been cleared up, Elizabeth, we should prepare ourselves for the séance."

"Agreed." She rose to her feet, and the two of them left as well. Henry didn't see if she looked at him or not; his gaze remained fixed on the door where Vincent had disappeared.

Where he had walked away and left Henry behind.

"Henry?" Jo asked softly.

"Go pack your things," he managed to say. They'd leave on the next train. Go back to Baltimore alone. Jo would stay with him, if only because she had little choice. But would she ever trust him again?

He'd destroyed everything, and for what? A moment of stupidity, compounded time and again by fear.

Jo touched his arm as she slipped past him. He waited until she was gone, then sank into his chair and wept.

Vincent's hands shook as he pulled his best coat from the clothespress. Impractical for wearing in the woods, but he didn't care. His stomach rolled with nausea, and bile burned the back of his throat.

How could Henry have done this to him? To all of them? God, he'd trusted the man, cared about him, given away his heart. And what had Henry given him in return? A pack of lies.

A soft knock came at his door. "Vincent?" Henry called. "Please, just let me explain."

Vincent's throat tightened, and he felt ill. He ignored Henry in favor of shucking off his vest. The dove gray would match the scarlet coat better. He should have set his shoes out for polishing earlier—what had he been thinking?

The door swung open behind him. "Vincent?"

"Get out." He didn't turn around, couldn't trust himself to look at Henry.

The door shut. "Please let me explain," Henry repeated, because of course the damned man couldn't listen, not once.

"Why?" Vincent turned to face him, and the sight of Henry's familiar face, his blue eyes wide and worried behind the lenses of his spectacles, physically hurt. "Why the hell should I listen to you, when you'll just lie to me again?"

"I won't, I swear." Henry took a step toward him.

Vincent stepped back, fetching up against the clothespress. "What else have you lied about?" A hot ball of bitter anger boiled in his chest. "Tell me. What else?"

"Nothing!" Henry held his hands out pleadingly. "Vincent, please, I swear. I never meant to hurt you."

"Then you failed." Henry flinched at the words, and a savage sort of satisfaction filled Vincent at the sight. "We're in *business* together, Henry. You, me, Lizzie, we all depend on each other, and here you are, pretending everything is fine, pretending the contacts and the backers are about to come through."

"I know!" Misery pooled in Henry's eyes. "You aren't telling me anything I haven't told myself. I'm sorry, Vincent, I was going to tell you, I was. But—"

"What else aren't you saying?" Vincent cut him off.

"Nothing!" Henry let his hands fall to his sides. "I'm not hiding anything else from you, but you won't believe it, will you?"

Vincent let out a bark of a laugh. "Don't you dare get angry with me."

"I wouldn't if you would just listen!"

Enough. He couldn't believe a word out of Henry's lying mouth. Bad enough he'd lied about the stupid Psychical Society, but what other deceptions might there have been? Vincent had thought himself Henry's only lover, and true, they'd made no promises, but how could he trust Henry even if they had?

"Get out," Vincent snapped, pointing at the door. "I'm done with you."

Henry's eyes widened as if he'd been slapped. "Vincent, no..."

"Get out!" The gleam of gold caught Vincent's eye, and he ripped free the cufflinks Henry had given him. He hurled them at Henry's head; Henry ducked and they struck the wall instead. "Get out! Go back to Baltimore! And take my name off your fucking sign!"

He stood still, chest heaving, teeth clenched. Henry stared at him for a long moment...then lowered his gaze. Leaving the cufflinks where they lay, he let himself out the door and shut it behind him.

Vincent closed his eyes, fighting for control. He wanted to keep throwing things—to break the mirror, to hurl the night candle against the wall. To rip the silver amulet from around his neck and scream a challenge to any ghost to come and take him if they could.

But he couldn't. Lizzie depended on him. Sylvester depended on him. And if Henry had shown himself false, all the more reason for Vincent to do his duty. Even if the only thing he really wanted to do was cry.

They made their way through the hot and uncomfortable woods, any stray breezes unable to penetrate the thick branches and choking undergrowth. The setting sun threw long shadows, which clustered beneath the trees, adding to the sense of oppression. Eyes seemed to stare from every hollow trunk, every patch of deep shade, but the taste of ashes had yet to manifest on Vincent's tongue.

He trudged along the rail line behind Sylvester and Lizzie, his heart slowing his steps as much as the unaccustomed exertion. The argument with Henry had left him even more drained and dispirited than before. He couldn't stop thinking about it, or about that moment when he'd realized it was true, that Henry had lied to him. Lied to them all.

And for what? Some sort of bizarre attempt at self-aggrandizement? Surely he must have realized Vincent would inevitably find out. Why do such a thing?

It didn't matter. Sylvester's words returned to haunt him: "*And what is your role in Mr. Strauss's life? What is it really?*"

Not that of confidante, obviously. Or of equal business partner. Whatever role Vincent had thought he played, he'd been wrong.

The memory of Henry's tenderness last night teased him. How gentle Henry had seemed, how open. His first concern had been for Vincent. Was it all just a trick of some sort? But to what possible end?

Lizzie let out an audible sigh and dropped back to walk beside him. "Would it help to talk about it?"

Bad enough he looked like a fool in front of her and Sylvester, without having salt rubbed in the wound. "No."

"Henry…is sometimes an idiot," she said, ignoring his answer. "Heaven knows, I'll be the first to say so. He has a brilliant mind, but he does things without thinking them all the way through. Especially when it comes to interacting with other people."

"I'm not certain what part of 'no' I was unclear on," Vincent replied. Was he not allowed to keep even a shred of whatever dignity remained to him?

"I'm only suggesting we hear him out before we dissolve our business and part ways," Lizzie said. "It's a disappointment the Psychical Society won't come through with any backers, but we're no worse off financially than we were before."

"Do what you want, Lizzie. I'm finished."

"Vincent—"

"Vincent is right," Sylvester said, looking back at them over his shoulder. Wonderful. Now Vincent got to hear his love life—his stupidity—discussed by them both. So much for his dignity. "Elizabeth, this lie might seem like a small thing to you, but is it? The man asked you to rely on his devices, when he himself knew they were unreliable. At the very least he has no concern for your safety."

"Henry's devices work, Sylvester." Lizzie's step quickened, carrying her closer to Sylvester and leaving Vincent blessedly alone. "We've seen them in operation. The Psychical Society's opinion hardly changes the evidence of my own eyes."

Sylvester shook his head. The last light glinted on his brown hair, picking out the strands of gray. "Liars don't restrict themselves to a single falsehood. Even if you are right, what else has he lied about?"

And that was the heart of it. What other falsehoods had Henry spun for them? "Sylvester is right," he said. "Henry is a liar. Worse—he's a hypocrite. Remember how he reacted when he discovered neither of us went by the name we were born with?"

"I could hardly forget," Lizzie said with a scowl. "But don't you be a hypocrite either, Vincent Night. You didn't think Henry ought to be angry because you lied about your past, claiming yourself the child of a white man and an 'Indian princess' for God's sake."

"That was different," he objected. "I tell the story to make myself palatable to our employers, as you very well know. Henry lied to *us.*"

Sylvester cast him a sympathetic look. "I'm sorry, Vincent. I did my best to warn you."

"I know." He should have listened to Sylvester from the start, just as he would have listened to Dunne. "I'm sorry I ignored you."

"As for dissolving your business," Sylvester glanced at Lizzie, then back to Vincent. "My offer still stands. Come with me, once this is all over. I know you'll find Europe far more accommodating."

And it would put an ocean between himself and Henry. "Agreed."

Lizzie made a disgusted noise. Sylvester arched a brow at her. "You object?"

"Only to making rash decisions in the heat of the moment. I'd rather talk to Henry and give him the opportunity to explain. If Vincent still feels betrayed afterward—"

"And what else would I feel?" he demanded, fists curling. "Henry—"

"Calm down, both of you," Sylvester said, his authoritative voice cutting through the air like a blade. "We've no need to give Rosanna even more energy than she already has."

Knowing the older man was right, Vincent forced himself to take a few deep breaths. He needed to put Henry out of his mind for now, at least until after the séance. High emotion in a situation like this made things much more dangerous. If Lizzie got hurt because of his broken heart...

They emerged into the cleared space where the old town had stood. The fall roared like a sleepy lion, its sparkling waters reflecting the sunset. Crimson clouds covered the western sky, mingled with gold and the occasional splotch of dark blue. It would have been beautiful, if the bitterness inside Vincent hadn't poisoned it for him.

"Where shall we hold the séance?" he asked.

Lizzie paused and surveyed the scene. "As the sun isn't down yet— and hopefully we'll finish before it does set—we need somewhere dark."

"I know just the place," Sylvester said. "If I recall from my earlier exploration of the site, the church's receiving vault is still intact."

Vincent nodded. "I saw it when we returned Zadock's bones." Which of course had been Henry's idea.

Not all of Henry's ideas were bad, though. If he'd only *told* Vincent the night in the saloon with Christopher, they would have commiserated instead of celebrated. Everything would have been fine.

Wouldn't it? If he only knew why Henry did such a stupid thing…

It didn't matter. Forcing his mind back to the task at hand, Vincent followed Sylvester across the ragged, torn earth until they reached the vault.

Unlike modern stone receiving vaults, this one was built into the hillside, with earth heaped above it to form a low dome. A stone archway still stood strong, as did the solid iron of the old door. Heavy flakes of rust lay beneath the hinges, where the workers had forced it open, looking for any lingering bodies to take to the Devil's Walk cemetery. A key stood in the lock, appearing in much better condition than it should have.

"This surely wasn't exposed to a century of weather," Vincent said, touching it.

"No. I suspect it ended up in the church, along with the parish records," Sylvester said. "Leave it be for now."

The door opened almost quietly, thanks to a heavy application of oil and grease from the modern-day workers. The interior of the vault was simple, nothing more than a single, low-roofed room with thick stone walls. The weight of the earth had bowed them in slightly, but they seemed in no danger of collapse. There were no shelves to store coffins; either the deceased awaiting burial had been stacked, or the village had been too small to need much space for its dead.

Vincent lit a candle, while Lizzie and Sylvester arranged themselves on the slate-tiled floor. Ordinarily the séance would be performed in darkness, but since their purpose amounted to an interrogation of the spirit, they needed light to read the ghost's responses.

Given Rosanna's strength, Vincent doubted a single candle would do much to deter her anyway. He pulled the door to, shutting out the last lingering light of day and leaving behind only the candle's pale illumination.

"Please join hands," Lizzie instructed as he settled beside her.

Vincent and Sylvester both took hold of Lizzie's right hand, leaving her left free to write. Their other hands they clasped together. Lizzie set her pencil to the notepad, doodling in slow loops and whirls without meaning. "Spirit of Rosanna," Lizzie said in a clear, commanding voice. "My hand is prepared to write your words. Draw from the energy of this circle and direct my pencil as you will. I stand ready to receive you."

Vincent's skin prickled. Sylvester's hand was warm in his, as was Lizzie's. He found himself straining for any taste of ashes. Lizzie's breathing slowed as she slipped into trance, the scratch of her pencil against the paper almost monotonous.

Would it work? Would Rosanna even answer the summons?

Ashes in his mouth answered his speculation, accompanied with the rancid flavor of overdone pork. The light of the single candle turned blue, losing whatever warmth it had possessed. A chill passed over his skin, the air of the receiving tomb going from cool to icy.

The sound of the pencil against the paper changed, jagged and sharp, as the spirit seized control of Lizzie's hand. The fingers he held tensed, turned into iron claws, the nails pressed hard against his skin. The idle loops became words, scratched furiously into the notebook.

I AM HERE.

CHAPTER 14

HENRY SAT in his hotel room, hands folded between his knees and his head bent. He'd meant to start packing for the trip back to Baltimore, but the sight of his clothes hanging alone in the clothespress sent him reeling to the bed. He'd gotten used to having Vincent's shirts beside his in the wardrobe above the shop. But all he would ever see again would be what he beheld in this moment: his own dull suits, unenlivened by Vincent's presence. Just like every other part of his life now.

There came a soft knock on the door. "Henry?" Jo called.

Jo. God. He owed her an explanation. He'd betrayed her trust just as much as anyone's. "Come in," he said, even though a part of him would have preferred to hide beneath the bed and pretend he wasn't there.

She entered, but he kept his gaze fixed on his hands. It was easier than seeing the condemnation in her eyes.

She stopped a few feet away, the hem of her yellow dress just at the edge of his vision. "I don't understand," she said uncertainly. "You always say to tell the truth. To be honest. So why did you lie to us about the Psychical Society?"

He took a deep breath and let it out slowly. He owed her honesty, but it didn't make speaking the words any easier. "Fear," he said at last.

"Fear?" She sounded puzzled.

Henry took off his glasses and rubbed tiredly at his eyes. "After so many years, I thought...but they wouldn't accept Reyhome Castle as proof of anything but a failure. Without my interference, Vincent and Lizzie would have cleared the place easily enough, and Mr. Gladfield survived."

"That isn't true!" The heat in her voice caused him to look up. Her tawny face was fixed in an angry frown, and her fists clenched, as if she wished to pummel the society with her bare hands. "I was there, Henry. I saw what happened. As did Vincent and Lizzie. They wouldn't have gone into business with you if they shared Dr. Kelly's opinion."

"Perhaps," he said. "I don't know any more."

"Well I do." She crossed her arms. "What were you afraid of?"

"Everything." He shook his head. "Failure. Letting you down, letting Lizzie down. Proving myself unworthy to…everyone."

"Everyone meaning Vincent in this case," she guessed.

He put his spectacles back on and glared at her. "That isn't any of your business, young lady."

Jo arched a skeptical brow at him. "I'm not blind or stupid, Henry."

"No, you're a sixteen year old girl who knows nothing about these things."

"I know love when I see it," she shot back.

The air felt sucked out of the room, his lungs hollow. "I…"

Jo stared at him as though wondering how he could be so thick. "Mama and Daddy loved each other. You could tell, just from the way they looked at one another. The way they'd laugh or smile at some joke only they shared. I thought it was embarrassing." She shrugged. "Once they were gone, I'd have given anything to watch Daddy tickle Mama until she all but cried, or see the silly way he'd grin when she played their special song on the piano."

It hurt, to think Henry might have shared in those memories, had the family not turned their backs on his uncle for marrying a black woman. "I'm sorry, Jo. I wish I'd known them."

A wistful smile touched her mouth. "So do I. But that's not why I'm saying this." She sat down on the bed beside him, the mattress dipping under her slight weight. "I see the same thing between you and Vincent."

Jo had to be mistaken. It wasn't the same. He and Vincent had made no promises to one another.

But he would have, if Vincent had asked. Would have promised anything.

"It doesn't matter," he said, and found himself blinking back foolish tears. "I thought this haunting would give me the chance to prove myself. But as you can see, I managed to botch that as well."

Jo heaved a sigh. "Then go after him! Help Vincent and Lizzie confront the ghost in the woods."

Henry shook his head. If only things were as simple as she seemed to believe. "I think they made it very clear they don't want my help."

She let out a disgusted snort. "And you're going to let that stop you?"

"It isn't that easy," he snapped. "What do you expect me to do?"

"To prove yourself!" she shot back. "Not to Vincent, or Lizzie. You never needed to prove anything to them here. You already did it at Reyhome, and in the shop. The only person you need to prove anything to is you."

He started to argue, but caught himself. If something terrible happened to Vincent while he sat here wallowing in self pity, he'd never forgive himself.

It wouldn't win back Vincent's heart, he didn't delude himself of that. He'd already thrown away whatever fragile claim he might lay to Vincent's affections. But anything would be better than just sitting here, desperately hoping nothing bad happened to them.

"You're right." Henry rose to his feet. "Help me fit whatever we can into my pack."

"And what about me?" she asked.

"You're staying here." When she opened her mouth to protest, he gave her a quelling look. "Jo, no. I want you in your room, with salt on all the windows and the door. Keep a sharp lookout, but don't leave the room unless the building is on fire."

She stood up to face him. Even though the top of her head barely came to his chin, she glared up at him defiantly. "But you need my help!"

Henry put his hands on her shoulders. "Your safety is my responsibility. I've already encountered Rosanna in the woods during the day, and it was a terrifying experience. I won't take you to face her there at night."

The look on his face must have convinced her. "Fine. You can take my headlamp, if you want."

He considered it, but… "I can't carry the batteries and my pack on my back at the same time."

They put everything that might be useful into the pack: compass, ghost grounder, portable galvanometer, and a bag of salt. Henry took up a lantern. Jo walked with him to the hotel door, where he paused.

"Thank you," he said. "And stay safe. I love you, Jo."

She rolled her eyes. "I know, Henry. Now get moving. The ghost isn't going to wait all night."

Vincent's throat went dry, sticking as he swallowed against the taste of charcoal and fire. Across from him, Sylvester let out a little hiss of alarm. "She's angry," he murmured. "But...not at us?" He cleared his throat. "Spirit of Rosanna, we have questions to ask of you. Do you wish us to return the remains of your son?"

The pencil scratched wildly against the paper. Lizzie's eyes rolled back into her head, showing only white. Her teeth clenched.

YES.

"We want to give you peace," Sylvester said. "But you must tell us where he is buried."

IN THE JAR.

What the devil? Vincent glanced across at Sylvester, who frowned slightly. "What do you mean? What jar?"

I PUT THINGS IN THE JAR. NAILS. HAIR. HIS HEART.

Vincent gasped. "She...she put her baby's heart in a jar?"

Rather than a look of horror, elation spread across Sylvester's face. "Not just a jar. A necromantic talisman. You used the bond between your baby and his father to summon a spirit to kill Zadock."

Lizzie's nails pierced Vincent's skin, and he gasped in pain but didn't try to draw away. He couldn't break the circle, not now when they were so close to unraveling this mess.

YES.

Sylvester...smiled. "Rosanna, I command you to tell me where this jar is."

HIS GRIEF IS THE SAME AS MINE. HE TOOK THE JAR. AWOKE ME. TURNED MY SON'S HEART AGAINST ME.

What did any of it mean? "Turned her son's heart against her? But the child must be in the otherworld."

Sylvester's eyes widened. "She must mean literally. Someone found the jar, realized its use, and used it to summon and bind Rosanna. Even someone not a medium could do it—she was on this side of the veil and had a direct connection to the talisman. That's why she's attacking Devil's Walk. Not out of her own will, but because she's under the command of one of the living inhabitants." Admiration showed in his gaze. "My God, she must have had talent, to have created an object so powerful."

"His grief is the same as mine," Vincent repeated. "Heartbroken, left for another...no. Not jealousy. Henry was right. This is about grief for a dead child. A dead son." He met Sylvester's eyes. The blue flame of the candle reflected eerily in their depths. "Fitzwilliam. His son died in a wall collapse. Emberey said the ground shift caused it—Fitzwilliam must have blamed Norris for approving the site fit for building. And Brooks must have been the foreman on the work crew Fitzwilliam's son was in."

"And then we showed up, trying to stop Rosanna," Sylvester said. "Fitzwilliam tried to warn Mr. Strauss away. When that didn't work, he ordered her to attack us in the graveyard."

YES. ALL MUST DIE.

IT ENDS TONIGHT.

"Someone else," Vincent said. "She's after someone else. But who?"

"Surveyor, foreman…overseer?" Sylvester suggested. "Is that right, Rosanna? Are you being sent against Mr. Emberey tonight?"

IT IS TIME.

The candle flame suddenly roared to life, stretching up toward the ceiling like a blue streamer. Lizzie's nails tore into Vincent's hand, and he jerked back instinctively from the pain.

The circle broke.

Lizzie pitched forward, gasping great lungfuls of air. The flame died to a more ordinary size and reverted to a soft, orange glow. The freezing room began to warm once again. Swearing softly, Vincent wrapped his handkerchief around his bloody hand. "Lizzie? Are you all right?"

Sylvester leaned over and put a supportive hand to her arm. She pressed her fingers to her forehead and nodded. "Yes. I…did we get our answers?"

"Rosanna made a necromantic charm using the heart of her stillborn baby," Vincent said. He stood up and pushed open the door to let in some fresh air. The sun had set, probably at the very moment Rosanna ended the séance. "Someone—probably Fitzwilliam's son—found the jar she used and took it home. Now Fitzwilliam is using it to order Rosanna to murder everyone he blames for the death of his own son."

"Emberey?" she guessed.

"Maybe. Or maybe the whole damned town." God, Henry and Jo were there. "We have to return to Devil's Walk immediately!"

"Let's not panic," Sylvester said, holding up his hand. "I agree, we must return to the town and confront Mr. Fitzwilliam. We'll take the jar from him. It's what we do afterward which I want to speak to you about first."

"What do you mean?" Why did Sylvester want to have a discussion while Henry might be in danger?

And God, despite everything, despite all the lies and the pain, he still cared about Henry. If Henry died, it would break him, grind all the little pieces left of his heart into dust.

Vincent swallowed, trying not to imagine it. Henry would be fine, so long as they acted quickly enough. "We smash the jar to bits, rebury anything left of the baby here in the woods, and lay Rosanna to rest."

"That is one possibility," Sylvester said carefully. "I would prefer to make a different suggestion."

The look Sylvester had worn on his face during the séance...the one of elation. "You knew it was true all along," Vincent said. The world seemed to slip sideways. "The legend of her summoning a spirit. You expected to find some kind of necromantic talisman."

"Hoped, more like." Sylvester smiled wryly. "I didn't *know* anything. But if the stories were true, then yes, there would be some sort of object to bind the spirit. I've been searching for evidence all along. When we dug up Zadock's grave, I'd thought perhaps Rosanna had secreted it on his person, or in his coffin."

"Which is why you insisted on examining his remains yourself," Vincent guessed.

"Of course. I never imagined it was in the hands of the living, compelling Rosanna to attack."

"But why were you looking for it?" Lizzie rose to her feet, her face pale. "Sylvester, this thing is an abomination! Surely you don't mean to use it!"

"Oh," he said. "But I do."

Sylvester might as well have punched Vincent in the gut. "You can't."

"Dunne would never have agreed to this," Lizzie said. "Never."

"Oh my poor child," Sylvester said with a sad chuckle. "Of course he would have. He suggested it in the first place."

No air remained in the little room. No air remained in the world. "Dunne is dead," Vincent said. "He's been gone for a year. Don't you dare blame him for this."

"And don't you dare play the fool, Vincent Night." Sylvester's hazel eyes narrowed angrily. "I told you we had plans. A vision—a dream for a better world. I left New York to find everything we'd need, all the bits of knowledge scattered across the globe just waiting to be fitted together. But to do so, I needed access. Access to the libraries of the ancient houses, of the church. The funds to venture to the far corners of the earth, where men in grass huts hold secrets that would shake the foundations of the civilized world.

"For twenty years, it worked. I became the Great Ortensi. But now? Now there's gray in my hair." His lip curled. "Clairsentience is too tame a talent, especially when combined with the aging body of a man. The new darlings of the spiritualist world are girls, nubile and soft. Not to mention willing to perform partially unclothed, to 'prove they have nothing hidden on their persons' or whatever excuse they come up with. I cannot compete. My last European tour was canceled halfway through due to lack of interest."

Lizzie eyed him warily. "I'm sorry, Sylvester, but it doesn't excuse the use of necromancy. None of this has anything to do with Dunne."

"Oh, but it does. He's the one who suggested I find a necromantic talisman—not to kill, merely to command. The feats I'd be able to order the spirits to perform would astonish. My career would be saved, and I'd have the opportunity to gather the last few pieces we needed. Unfortunately, it's taken almost two years for me to find a genuine talisman."

"No." Lizzie shook her head. "Dunne would never have agreed to such a thing."

"He should have told you, when you survived your apprenticeships." Sylvester arched his brow. "Or did you truly think you were the first?"

"We were," Vincent said, but his lips went numb. "He took Lizzie in. Then me. There was no one else."

"And I suppose you also believe he scooped you up out of the gutter for no other reason outside the goodness of his heart?" Sylvester's look became pitying. "James did have a good heart—of course he did. You saw it for yourselves. He donated to every charity, gave a coin to every beggar. But the two of you were chosen. Special. Why do you believe he brought you into his house, instead of taking you to the orphanage or handing you a coin? Why else did he raise and train you, give everything of himself to make you better mediums?"

Vincent swayed. It was all lies. Sylvester spun a wild story in order to justify his own desire for fame. Nothing more.

"If James still lived, we'd all be together now," Sylvester said gently. "He would have done an infinitely better job of explaining things than I have."

"I imagine so, as you've explained nothing!" Lizzie chopped the air violently with her hand. "What are these plans of yours? Why should we go along with anything that includes necromancy?"

Sylvester glanced outside. "There's no time. We need to return to

Devil's Walk, before Fitzwilliam flees with the jar, or does it some harm after killing Emberey. For the moment, I can only beg that you trust me." He looked back at them. "And if my word isn't enough, trust James. Trust he had only the greater good in mind when he suggested this."

This wasn't happening. Vincent was trapped in some awful nightmare. Or else Sylvester was lying, or had gone mad, or…something. Anything, as long as his words about Dunne weren't true.

"We're supposed to look after the living and the dead," he said raggedly. "Whatever these plans of yours are, the price is too high. Necromancy means dragging the dead from their rest, forcing them back across the veil, and enslaving them to our will. It's against everything we stand for as mediums."

Lizzie stepped to his side. "Vincent is right, Sylvester. Now let's return to Devil's Walk and save Mr. Emberey. We'll talk afterward, if you want."

For a long moment, Sylvester said nothing, his gaze turned inward. Then he sighed. "I'm sorry, Elizabeth. I can't trust you not to destroy the jar out of some misguided ideals." He drew a wicked looking knife from inside his coat. "I'll need to ask you to remain here until after I've secured it."

The candle's reflection gleamed on the blade. Lizzie gasped, and Vincent pushed her behind him. "You—you won't kill us. Not if we're important to your plans."

Sylvester actually looked hurt. "I won't kill you because I love you, my boy," he said. "But I will hurt you, if I must. This is so much bigger than just us."

Neither of them moved. Sylvester backed to the door. "I'll come back for you, as soon as this is ended," he promised, and swung it closed behind him. There came the sound of the key turning in the lock.

They were trapped.

CHAPTER 15

HENRY TRIPPED over a rail tie and swore angrily. The sun had gone down, and the wind began to howl. The branches of the trees swayed and thrashed against the sky. The light of his lantern barely illuminated the track well enough for him to see the rail bed in front of him, and he stumbled over every uneven tie. His heavy pack pulled on his left shoulder; after all the exercise of the last few days, its ordinary dull ache flared into a continuous thread of pain.

What if he was too late? He should have insisted on accompanying them earlier, not wallowed in his guilt. What if Rosanna possessed Lizzie completely, or set fire to them all, or…

No. He couldn't think like that.

A faint light winked at him through the trees.

Henry froze. Was it a lantern? Did the others return already?

Or was it Rosanna, trying to lure him to his doom?

Instinct prodded him off the railroad track and into the trees beside it. Shuttering his lantern, he crouched down and waited. A pouch of salt hung at his belt; if Rosanna appeared, he'd fling it at her and run for his life. Or could he use the iron rails to ground her somehow?

The light came into view once again. It belonged to a lantern, not a ghostly woman. But its light shone only on Ortensi's face.

Where were Lizzie and Vincent? Behind Ortensi, lost in the shadows? But the tracks were treacherous at night—they would surely need to see where they were going if they didn't want to break an ankle.

Something was very wrong.

Henry all but held his breath as Ortensi drew nearer, irrationally certain the medium would sense his presence amidst the trees. But he was no spirit, and Ortensi hurried past without so much as glancing in his direction.

Henry waited until the light vanished before unshuttering his lantern again. His heart pounded against his ribs as he climbed back to the tracks. What had happened to Vincent and Lizzie? Why would Ortensi return to the town without them?

Did the ghost kill them both?

Oh God. No. Bile coated at the back of his throat. His lungs couldn't get enough air. What if Rosanna succeeded this time, without Jo or Henry to interfere? Set Lizzie aflame, dashed Vincent's brains out, or burned him too…

Henry broke into a run. He had to see for himself. Had to get to them. He wouldn't believe it until he saw their dead bodies.

"Vincent," he whispered, like a mantra. "I'm coming, Vincent. Hold on, wherever you are, whatever's happening. Please don't leave me."

A few minutes later, he stumbled into the great clearing. The beams of the mill clawed at the night sky, like the fingers of a skeletal hand. "Vincent!" he shouted between pants for breath. "Lizzie! Where are you?"

There came no reply, only the shriek of the wind through the trees.

He ran through the site, tripping over boards, ducking through scaffolding, shining his light wildly about. But there was no sign of either of them.

"Vincent!" he shouted again and again, until his throat was raw. The wind ate his words, flung them back in his face.

He staggered to a halt, gasping. He had to find them. But how? They could be anywhere in this God-forsaken woods. He needed help.

Help.

Hands shaking, he slipped the straps from his shoulders and opened the pack. Taking out the portable galvanometer, he stared at the dial. "Rosanna!" he shouted. "You asked for my help, and I want to give it to you! But I can't unless you show me where Vincent and Lizzie are!"

The dial remained still. It wouldn't work. Of course it wouldn't—it would be as useless as everything else he'd done since coming to Devil's Walk

The gauge suddenly jerked to the right. A pulse.

An acknowledgement?

He turned to the right, and the reading died back. All but holding his breath, he turned in the other direction and took a step toward the old church.

The field strength increased, sending the gauge to the right.

"Yes," he said. "Thank you, Rosanna. Now lead me to them."

Vincent leaned his back against the stacked stone wall of the receiving vault, his legs stretched out before him. Lizzie sat opposite, her arms laced around her knees and her head bowed. The candle burned between them, but soon its light would go out.

Vincent had wasted half an hour desperately seeking some method of escape. Prying at the edge of the frame where iron met stone, attempting to loosen the mortar around it, and finally pounding on the door and shouting himself hoarse. He might still be doing the latter, had Lizzie not ordered him to sit down and stop giving her a headache with the noise.

"Do you think Sylvester's telling the truth?" Vincent asked. "About...about Dunne."

And about us, he wanted to add. But the words stuck in his throat. What did he say to Henry, about never knowing what Dunne saw in him?

"...*a boy with a good heart,*" Henry said. And Vincent had wished it true.

He wished it even more now.

Lizzie shook her head slowly. "I don't want to believe it. But that doesn't make it a lie."

"It has to be." Vincent wouldn't—couldn't believe anything else. "Sylvester's gone mad. Dunne would never condone this, let alone suggest it to him in the first place. Never. And there certainly weren't any other apprentices, especially not ones who came to some dubious end."

Lizzie said nothing. Vincent shifted his foot and prodded her ankle. "Right?"

"I don't know."

He felt as though the ground had opened up, and he balanced on the last solid ledge above the abyss. "Dear God. You haven't been lying about anything too, have you?"

"Of course not!" Her head snapped up, revealing a face streaked with tears. "But something happened that I haven't thought of in years until tonight."

He wasn't certain he could take many more revelations. "What?"

"I found a chest in the attic."

She must be misremembering things. "My room was in the attic."

"Eventually, yes. This was before you. Perhaps a month after Dunne rescued me. He went out, and left me alone. I was horribly bored, having been bedridden since I arrived. My leg had finally healed enough for me to hobble around. I was so sick of lying in bed, I was willing to put up with the pain just to move about some. So I took the opportunity to explore the rooms of the house I hadn't seen yet, and ended up in the attic."

Her arms tightened around her knees. "What would become your furniture was already there—clearly someone used it as a bedroom before. But there were other things—trunks and the like. They were full of personal belongings: hairbrushes, clothing, novels. Some of the clothes belonged to a girl. Dunne came back and found me trying on hats in the mirror."

"Were you frightened?" he asked softly. "When he discovered you, I mean."

"Not in the least." A wistful smile trembled on her lips. "I'd say it was because he already knew. I gave him the whole sorry story when he offered to take me to his house, bandage my wounds, and set my broken bones. But truthfully, I never feared Dunne. Not for a single second."

Neither had Vincent. Not really, not in the way he'd feared so many other men. "What happened then?"

Lizzie stared at the flame; it flickered in the depths of her haunted gaze. "He said I should take whatever I liked. I asked him who the things belonged to, and he said the previous owners of the house left the trunks. He'd simply never gotten rid of them. The next time I went into the attic they were gone. I assumed he'd finally had them removed, but..."

She didn't finish. Didn't have to, because they were both thinking the same thing. Sylvester had used the word *survived* when it came to their apprenticeships.

There had been tense moments, dangerous ones even, in their training as mediums. But Dunne would never have let anything truly bad happen to them.

Would he?

"We can't worry about it now," Vincent said, tipping his head back to stare blankly at the ceiling. "If Fitzwilliam hasn't already summoned Rosanna to kill Emberey, he will soon." Assuming he didn't mean to wipe out the entire town.

"Unless you have some way of getting us out of here, I don't see what we can do about it." Lizzie bowed her head again. "We're trapped. There's nothing to do but wait for Sylvester to come back."

"And then what?"

She glanced up at him. "That depends on what happens to Henry and Jo."

Vincent closed his eyes. God, he'd been angry with Henry. Angry with *himself* for trusting someone who didn't deserve it.

No wonder Sylvester had seemed set against Henry from the start. It had nothing to do with Henry's idiotic falsehood. It was all about the necromantic talisman. Sylvester surely didn't want any more people to know about such a thing than absolutely necessary. Certainly not if his great comeback were to succeed. No one could know his renewed powers came from necromancy rather than simple talent.

Vincent and Lizzie weren't just a part of whatever scheme Sylvester and Dunne—no, Sylvester alone—had hatched. They were the closest thing Sylvester had to family. But Henry was an outsider. The modernity of his methods, the fact he wasn't a medium, must have made him seem even more of a potential threat. Vincent revealing Henry spent the night in his bed certainly hadn't helped.

So Sylvester set out to separate Vincent from Henry, beginning on the first day. And it worked, thanks to Henry's absurd lie about his reception at the Psychical Society.

As long as Henry didn't find out about the jar, he'd be safe. If he remained in the hotel and kept his head down, and let Sylvester and Fitzwilliam battle things out...

Which he'd never do because, well, he was Henry. He'd run out at the first sign of the ghost, waving his rod around.

He'd be on hand to see what Sylvester did with the jar, and notice Vincent and Lizzie were absent. And either Sylvester would come up with some very clever explanation...

Or once the jar was in his hands, he'd let Rosanna deal with Henry.

Vincent wanted to leap to his feet. To dig through the weight of earth above them, run through the forest, and save Henry and Jo. Carry his little family away from here, from Sylvester and the ghost and every danger.

His family.

Why didn't he at least give Henry the chance to explain? Maybe Henry had lied about other things, but at least Vincent could have waited to find out why Henry had spun his falsehood about the society. Instead he'd screamed and thrown away his cufflinks, and refused to let Henry speak.

He'd wanted Henry to hurt, just as much as he'd been hurting.

What had Lizzie said earlier, about knowing Henry's devices worked? Why hadn't Vincent set aside his pride and overridden Sylvester? Insisted Henry come with them to make some sort of amends by lending his assistance?

Why had he been such a fool?

A heavy fist banged against the door. "Vincent? Lizzie? It's Henry!"

Vincent stared blankly. It wasn't. It couldn't be.

Unlike him, Lizzie didn't remain frozen in shock. Lurching to her feet, she ran to the door and struck it herself. "Henry! We're in here!"

"Thank God!" came the muffled shout. "Hold on a moment, and I'll get you out!"

"How? Sylvester took the key!" she shouted back.

"An old lock like this should be simple to pick. Just give me a moment to get out some wire."

Vincent wanted to laugh aloud—partly in relief to have Henry here and unharmed, and partly because *of course* Henry would recognize an older lock. He swallowed it back, not certain if the laugh would emerge amused or hysterical.

Within short order, there came a click, and the door swung open. Vincent scrambled to his feet. Lizzie said nothing, merely flung her arms around Henry. Startled, he patted her awkwardly on the back. "Er…"

"I've never been so glad to see you." She let go and stepped back. "But what are you doing here?"

"Jo suggested I come and see if I could offer assistance, actually," he said.

"She's a smart girl." Her mouth flattened. "Sylvester locked us in."

"I saw him going back to town alone." Henry shifted the pack on his back. "I knew something had to be wrong, so I hid, then came here to look for you."

"Good work, Henry." She stepped outside. "Coming, Vincent?"

Vincent didn't move, his gaze fixed on Henry. His heart beat in his throat, and he didn't know what to say, what to feel.

"I…" Henry trailed off and looked away, his face crumpling. "I know you aren't happy to see me, Vincent."

But he was. If only he could make his tongue work.

"I don't blame you," Henry went on. "And I know this doesn't make up for things somehow. I lied and…" His breath caught. "I'm sorry. I was so humiliated. And when I saw you with Christopher Maillard, I lost my head."

"Christopher?" Vincent exclaimed, shocked back into mobility. "What the devil does Christopher have to do with anything?"

Henry's mouth tightened. "I heard what he said. About composing poetry in praise of your *performance.*"

"I don't think I want to hear this," Lizzie said, and moved farther away from the door.

Vincent's head spun. "Wait a moment. You thought I'd slept with Christopher?"

"Of course!" Fire flashed briefly in Henry's eyes. "Do you think I'm a fool? I know I'm not...not the sort of man you'd usually find interesting. Not an aesthete, or a poet, or a musician." He swallowed convulsively. "I'm just boring old Henry. And when I saw him there, all but throwing it in my face that he'd had you—"

"Dear God, are you mad?" Vincent stared at Henry aghast. "Christopher is in love with the sound of his own voice. Didn't I go home with you that night?"

"Because you thought I was worth something!" Henry shouted. He turned his head to the side, as if he couldn't bear to look at Vincent. "Because I *lied.* You sacrificed so much to move, to go into business with me, and I couldn't even hold your attention in the bedroom." A tear sparked in the candlelight. "I just wanted you to love me."

All the air seemed sucked out of the vault. Vincent took a step forward, then stopped, feeling as though both of them might shatter at the slightest touch.

"Of course I love you," he said.

Henry lifted his head, eyes wide. "You do?" he asked, although it was more a sob than words.

Vincent didn't remember crossing the space between them. "Oh, Henry." He wrapped his arms tight around his lover. "Of course I do. Why else do you think I was so angry with you?"

Henry's hands gripped his coat, crushing the velvet, but Vincent couldn't bring himself to care. "But you...but I...we never...and Christopher..."

"Then let me say it now. I haven't been with anyone else since we met—and I hope never to be again." And oh God, it was terrifying, to leave himself exposed like this, the most tender parts of his heart laid bare.

"I never slept with Christopher—never so much as kissed him,"

Vincent went on. "And—and I feared you'd grown tired of me, or found out the society refused my application."

"They did what?" And of course, of all the things to get Henry's attention, that would be the one.

Vincent sighed. "I...wasn't entirely honest with you, either. I did apply, but they rejected me. I didn't say anything because I knew their support might still be valuable."

Henry tried to pull free, but Vincent refused to allow it. Henry settled for glowering at him. "And why did they refuse you?"

Vincent barely restrained himself from rolling his eyes. "You-um guess-um, chief."

Henry released a blistering stream of invective. "Mother fucking sons of whores," he finished. "If I'd known, I'd have told them to shove my presentation up their asses!"

"A lady is present!" Lizzie yelled from outside. "And what are you two doing? We have to get to the town! Sylvester and Rosanna are likely both there now."

Damn it. Vincent pulled Henry roughly against him. "I'm sorry," he said. "I never meant you to feel as though I was anything less than yours. And if you can forgive my lie of omission, I'll forgive your outright one."

"Hmph," Henry snorted into his shoulder. "We'll have to revisit your standards of honesty, Vincent Night. But...yes. God, yes." He tipped his head back, his eyes vulnerable behind the glass shield of his spectacles. "I love you, Vincent."

Vincent kissed him tenderly. "I love you, too," he whispered, and the words sent a thrill through him, to be spoken aloud. "And I can't wait to show you how much. But right now, we have a town to save."

CHAPTER 16

THEY LEFT the receiving vault and headed for the rail line. Vincent and Lizzie started to turn south, back toward Devil's Walk, but Henry called, "No! There's a faster way!"

They halted. Vincent's black hair fell into his eyes, and for some reason the sight did strange things to Henry's heart.

Vincent loved him. Loved *him,* despite all the stupid things he'd said and done. It seemed almost like a dream, except presumably a dream would have included less agonizing betrayal and fewer articles of clothing.

"What do you mean?" Vincent asked, when Henry didn't continue.

Henry told himself to focus and gestured to the end of the rail spur. A group of flat cars sat there, some of them still loaded with brick and iron beams. "We ride the rails, of course."

Vincent arched a brow. God, even dirty and exhausted, he looked handsome in his crimson coat and tailored trousers. "The one flaw in your plan would be the lack of an engine to pull them."

"It's downhill until we reach Devil's Walk," Henry replied, making for the cars. "We'll uncouple the first one and ride it down."

Lizzie laughed. "Brilliant, Henry. Perhaps we'll get lucky and run down Sylvester on the way."

She climbed onto the first flat car, which had been unloaded before the workers deserted the site. Henry handed his pack up to her, then uncoupled the car from the one behind it. "All right, Vincent. Remove the chocks. We might have to give it a shove to get it started."

Vincent pulled the chocks free, and Henry pushed as hard as he could. To his surprise, it took little effort to get the flat car rolling. Vincent scrambled onto it, then reached down. "Run, Henry!"

Henry jumped for the car. Vincent grabbed his arm and the back of his coat, hauling him onto the scarred wood platform. They fell back in a tangle of limbs.

"Got you," Vincent said with a grin.

"That you do."

Vincent's grin softened, and he swept a kiss across Henry's lips, before shoving at his chest. "We should probably sit up."

As the incline grew steeper, the car began to go faster, rushing down rails gleaming silver in the moonlight. The wind tore at Henry's hair, his hat long gone. Lizzie perched near the front of the car, peering forward, as if she could make Ortensi appear before them. Vincent stayed at the rear with Henry, their thighs pressed together. Henry took his hand, felt Vincent's fingers curl in his.

"Tell me what happened," he said over the wind. "What did you find out? And why did Ortensi lock you and Lizzie in the receiving vault?"

It wasn't easy to hear over the wind, so Vincent leaned against him, speaking almost into his ear. Under ordinary circumstances, Henry would have enjoyed sitting there so close, with Vincent's head resting against his shoulder. Now, though, he had the urge to throttle Ortensi with the man's own silk necktie.

"He was lying," he said, when Vincent finished. "You knew Dunne far better than he. There was no—no plan, or whatever absurdity the man claims."

Vincent's black eyes gleamed, suspiciously bright in the moonlight. "I hope you're right. I still can't believe Sylvester would stoop to necromancy, no matter the cause."

Henry had no trouble believing it...but he wasn't precisely unbiased, either. "What do you intend to do?"

"Keep him away from the accursed jar. Destroy the thing. After, I'm not sure." Vincent pressed closer, as if for comfort. "It isn't as if he's committed some crime."

"What's to stop him from finding another artifact, or learning to make one himself?"

"Nothing," Vincent said, not bothering to hide his bitterness. "But right now, we have to worry about what Sylvester might do tonight, not some unspecified future. Look—there's the town. I hope you gave some thought to stopping the flat car?"

"We should lose momentum—the track levels out well before the depot." Henry peered toward the town. "I don't see any smoke, at least. Fitzwilliam must not have made his move just yet."

The flat car began to slow, gradually at first, then more noticeably. Eventually it glided to nearly a stop. Henry jumped off, followed by Vincent. Lizzie tossed Henry his pack, then hopped down into Vincent's arms.

Only a few lights showed in the village. "Where is Fitzwilliam's house?" Lizzie asked, brushing off her skirts.

"I've no idea." Henry glanced at Vincent, got a shake of the head in return. "Curse it."

"Emberey will know," Lizzie said. "He's the target of the ghost—someone needs to protect him while the rest deal of us with Fitzwilliam. And…and Sylvester."

"Henry!" Jo shouted.

He spun—what was she doing out here? She ran toward them, a lantern in one hand and a satchel in the other. Its yellow light revealed a look of fear on her face.

"Are you all right?" she cried. "I thought something terrible had happened!"

Startled, he caught her in his arms. "I'm all right, Jo. Why did you think something went wrong?"

"Mr. Ortensi came back alone. I spotted him through the hotel window. I ran out and asked where you were. He said he hadn't seen you. I thought you didn't make it through the forest." She hefted the satchel. "I was coming to save you."

Henry hugged her tightly. "I appreciate the rescue. Ortensi is a traitor. He imprisoned Vincent and Lizzie."

"And if he knows Henry went into the woods after us, Sylvester must realize there's a chance Henry let us out," Vincent said. His expression was flat, but his fist clenched. "He's probably run straight to Fitzwilliam's house, assuming he knows where it is."

"Curse it." Henry released Jo. "Stay close. We're going to Mr. Emberey's house."

The square lay silent, save for the chime of the clock tower. Most of the houses showed no light. Given their relatively impressive facades, it seemed likely the owners possessed wealth enough to leave town until the danger was past.

It made the lone sliver of light spilling out from one even more noticeable. Had someone left a door ajar?

"Isn't that Emberey's house?" Lizzie asked sharply.

Vincent let out a hiss. "She's here. Rosanna is here!"

Vincent ran for the open door, his mouth full of ashes and rancid flesh. There was no time for subtlety; he kicked the door hard, sending it crashing back against the wall. "Emberey!" he shouted. "Em—"

He stumbled to a halt. Emberey stood at the bottom of the stairs leading to the second floor. Before him, shabby coat and dirty shoes looking out of place in the large foyer, stood Fitzwilliam.

And at Fitzwilliam's side burned Rosanna.

Fitzwilliam clutched a small earthenware jar in his hands. His face twisted in a look of fury, his eyes wild and staring. "Stay back!" he shouted. His voice turned to steam in the icy air. Rosanna turned her head, ghostly tendons and vertebrae snapping loudly, until her ruined eyes stared at them.

"Help!" shouted Emberey. His ivory skin went paper white with fear. "Stop him! He's mad!"

"I'm the sanest person in this damned town!" Fitzwilliam growled. "You and your kind let our sons die to build your mills and factories, but does anyone stand up to you the way they should? No! Your filthy money bought their souls."

A manic smile touched his face, terrible to see. Vincent shuddered. "When my boy brought me the jar he'd found in the diggings, I knew it must be God's will. My ancestor was only a girl when Whispering Falls burned, but she remembered seeing the witch whispering to the jar, one day when she played in the woods. She wrote about it in her diary, many years later. And as soon as I touched it, I knew this was the same jar."

Did the man have some mediumistic talent, too small to channel spirits, but enough to sense such a powerful artifact? Perhaps it ran in their line, and had prompted his son to pick up the accursed thing in the first place.

"At the time I didn't know it was put in my hands to do God's work," Fitzwilliam went on. "To cleanse this modern-day Gomorrah, starting with the three devils who let my boy die. You're going to pay for your sins, Emberey. I'm here to watch you burn."

Rosanna's gaze returned to the fore. In eerie silence, she began to drift toward Emberey.

In the seconds it took to wrest the jar from Fitzwilliam, Emberey might die. Vincent darted forward, past Fitzwilliam. "Get the jar!" he shouted over his shoulder. Pulling the bag of salt from inside his coat, he wrenched it open.

Emberey screamed in terror, scrambling madly up the stairs. Rosanna's flames burned stronger, and she let out her piercing shriek. Emberey screamed again, clutching his ears.

"I'm sorry, Rosanna!" Vincent said, and hurled the contents of the salt bag onto her.

She vanished in a swirl of ectoplasm. "You did it!" Emberey exclaimed.

"It won't last more than a few seconds." Vincent grabbed the man's arm. "Run for the door—we don't want her burning the house down around us. I—"

Rosanna materialized inches from Vincent.

Her blow sent him skidding down the stairs and onto the floor. Emberey's boots thudded past a second later, making for the door.

"No!" shouted Fitzwilliam, and Henry let out a cry of pain.

Vincent rolled to his elbow and looked up the stairs. Rosanna drifted down toward him, her fiery hair and dress streaming behind her.

The flames spread, racing over the floor and up the walls. They burned blue in her presence, the spectral light at odds with the heat pouring forth. Vincent stumbled to his feet, beginning to cough as smoke billowed from the burning wallpaper. He turned his back on her and made for the door.

Henry lay on the floor, blood trickling down the side of his face. Jo crouched beside him, wiping at it with her handkerchief.

"Henry!" Vincent stumbled to them.

Henry blinked. "Fitzwilliam—he hit me in the head with the jar."

"He ran after Mr. Emberey," Jo said. Something caught her attention over Vincent's shoulder, and her eyes went wide. "Vincent! Duck!"

He flung himself to the floor. A blast of hot air roared over them, and he glimpsed Rosanna flash past, like a spark on the wind. For a moment he thought the house would come down on their heads. Then the flames turned hot orange—she'd left, in pursuit of Emberey.

"Where is Lizzie?" he asked. Smoke stung his eyes, and he blinked rapidly in an attempt to clear them.

"She went after Fitzwilliam," Jo said. "We have to get out of here!"

"Go!" Vincent ordered. He hauled Henry to his feet. Smoke billowed around them, and Henry began to cough. Vincent dragged

Henry out the door and into the clean night air.

Lizzie leaned against the side of the house, her free hand on her ribs. "Sylvester," she said, before Vincent could ask. "The bastard lay in wait outside. He knocked me into the wall."

"Look!" Jo exclaimed, pointing.

The light of the flames washed over Devil's Walk, illuminating the square. Rosanna burned like a second fire, advancing once again on Emberey. The overseer fell to the ground, either from injury or terror.

Not fifteen feet away, Fitzwilliam and Sylvester struggled over the jar.

Both clutched its earthenware body, each striving to wrench it from the other's grasp. Fitzwilliam's lips drew back from his teeth, his expression utterly deranged. "Emberey must pay! Must atone for his sins!" he howled.

Sylvester kicked him in the shin. Fitzwilliam staggered, and Sylvester almost succeeded in yanking the jar free. With an incoherent snarl, Fitzwilliam snapped his head forward, smashing his forehead into Sylvester's face.

Sylvester let go and staggered away, blood running freely from his nose.

"Henry, Lizzie—take your salt and use it on Rosanna," Vincent said, and made for Fitzwilliam.

Fitzwilliam started to turn at the sound of Vincent's footsteps—but not fast enough. Praying his companions held Rosanna off Emberey for just a few more minutes, he launched himself at Fitzwilliam.

There was no finesse to it. They both went down in the mud. The sleeve of Vincent's coat gave at the seam. Fitzwilliam's elbow cracked audibly against a stone embedded in the muck.

And the jar went flying.

The air pressure changed instantly, Vincent's ears popping. Fitzwilliam made it to his knees, so Vincent kicked the jar, sending it skidding away from Fitzwilliam's grasp. Then he rolled away, even as heat bloomed behind him.

Henry grabbed Vincent and pulled him up. "Emberey—" Vincent gasped.

"She's not after him anymore," Henry said, his eyes wide with horror.

Vincent followed his gaze. Fitzwilliam managed to get to his feet, but the jar had vanished into the shadows somewhere. Rosanna stood before the man who had bound her, even as she bound some other unfortunate spirit all those years ago.

"St-stay away!" he shouted, backing up.

She screamed. Every window facing the square shattered, and the sound buzzed in Vincent's teeth as much as in his ears. Fitzwilliam cringed away, arms flung up, as if he could somehow ward her off.

She stretched her hand out and grabbed his arm. Flames poured out from her. His clothing caught, hair igniting, and now he was the one screaming.

"Don't watch, Jo," Henry said. She hid her face in his chest, hands pressed over her ears.

Vincent froze to the spot, transfixed by horror. Fitzwilliam's cries died away, and he collapsed to the ground. His body twitched once or twice, and then remained still. The stench of burning cloth and hair, of charring flesh, washed over them, joining the taste in Vincent's mouth until he nearly gagged. Beside him, Lizzie turned and vomited.

Rosanna turned away from the smoldering pile that was all which remained of Fitzwilliam. Her boiled-egg eyes seemed to seek out Vincent. "Bring him back," she said in a voice of flame and wind.

Vincent nodded. "I will."

She vanished. For a long moment, all was silent save for the crackling of the burning house behind them. Then Sylvester spoke.

"I'm afraid you won't be able to keep your promise, Vincent," he said, and held up the earthenware jar.

Vincent was painfully aware of his heart beating in his ears. The world seemed to slow, just as it had at the receiving vault. Sylvester stared back at him, blood dripping slowly from his nose and onto the jar. He didn't even seem to notice.

"Damn it," Sylvester said. "I told you two I'd explain everything. Why didn't you wait?" His gaze slid from Vincent to Henry, and his expression shifted to one of contempt. "Of course. Mr. Strauss convinced you to come and try to stop me."

"You locked us in!" Lizzie exclaimed.

"For your own good!" Sylvester met Vincent's gaze. "Vincent, my boy. You said you fear the ghost that killed James might return to possess you again." He lifted the jar slightly. "I can stop it. Send it back to whatever hell it crawled out of, and free you from a lifetime of looking back over your shoulder."

Vincent swallowed convulsively. "Even if it does return—even if it kills me—how can you justify this? You clearly meant to wait until after

Fitzwilliam murdered Emberey before taking the jar from him."

"You're fired, Ortensi," Emberey barked. He was covered in mud from his fall, and still dreadfully pale, but clearly his encounter had left him no worse for wear. "I don't know what this jar is, but hand it over, and I might not have you thrown in jail."

Sylvester's lip curled. "Look at him, Vincent. A small-minded penny pincher, who would gladly see men die if it saves the company a bit of money." He glanced at Henry again. "And your Mr. Strauss—a man with a soul of wheels and gears, an arrogant liar." His gaze returned to Vincent. "Your life is worth both of theirs put together. Do you really think this is what Dunne wanted for you?"

Above them, the clock tower's bell began to ring. Twelve strokes. Midnight.

"To hell with this," Emberey snarled, and started for Sylvester.

"No," Vincent said, but it was too late.

Sylvester closed his eyes and laid his hand on the jar. The air turned to ice, and Vincent's ears popped painfully. Strange flavors assaulted his tongue, one atop the next atop the next: apples and candy, whiskey and gunpowder, blood and bile and bitter wormwood.

A man like Fitzwilliam, with no real mediumistic talent of his own, could summon only a spirit already connected to the jar. Rosanna, who had made it, and whose blood ran in the heart of her son.

But a true medium like Sylvester? The reach it gave him was far, far greater.

Ectoplasm rolled like mist in the air as ghosts struggled to manifest. Dear God, how many had Sylvester summoned?

Emberey shrank back, his eyes wide with terror as the figure of an old man flickered into being between him and Sylvester. Vincent didn't think, just ran forward and seized Emberey's arm, dragging him back. "Leave this place and trouble us no more!" he ordered, putting all the power he could into the command.

The ghost shivered and vanished—and reappeared as Sylvester dragged it back from the otherworld.

"Stop this foolish defiance!" Sylvester shouted at him. "Leave them, come with me, and let me explain things to you!"

"Nothing can explain this!" Vincent said. Sylvester had raised the ghosts of Devil's Walk, dragged the spirits of those who died here back into this world without their consent.

Grief twisted Sylvester's face. "I'm sorry it came to this."

Unseen hands snatched at Vincent, shoving and hitting. He

staggered, and Emberey cried out in pain.

Lizzie grabbed his arm. "Run!" she shouted, and dragged him after her.

He ran blindly, hauling Emberey along with him. Henry and Jo fled in front of them, and behind, the ghosts swirled into being. His boots slipped on the frost gathering on the stones and mud of the square, but he kept his feet.

The clock tower loomed above them. Henry flung open the door, and Jo ran in, followed by the rest. The tower sat atop a large, square room. To one side, metal stairs led up into the clock tower proper. To the other was a boiler and some machinery whose purpose Vincent couldn't guess. Arc lamps hung from the ceiling, no doubt intended to illuminate the interior, but they were cold and dark.

"Salt!" Henry shouted, and slammed the door as soon as Vincent and Emberey ran through. Henry dropped his pack and pulled a salt bag from it, dumping the contents in a hasty line across the doorway. Jo did the same with the windowsills, using a bag from her satchel. Lizzie joined them, and within a few moments everything was sealed.

Emberey backed slowly away from the door, his expression frozen in a mask of horror. "W-Will it keep them back?"

"Yes. As long as the salt isn't disturbed." Vincent cautiously peered out the window.

The dead pressed against the glass. Ectoplasm began to form, a swirl of sickly light. Cold eyes glowed like a hundred tiny candles, their flames a horrid shade of greenish yellow.

"What do we do?" Emberey asked anxiously. "Do we wait for dawn?"

A flame kindled behind the rows of dead, coalescing into the shape of a woman. "Damn it," Vincent said. "He's called back Rosanna."

"She can break glass," Emberey said, backing up even farther.

"It isn't the glass holding them back," Lizzie replied. Her face was drawn and tense as she joined Vincent at the window. "But without it, a strong enough wind could disrupt the salt. Or rain dissolve it, should we be truly unlucky."

Vincent stared at the flaming ghost as she slowly stalked closer. He'd thought Sylvester wouldn't kill them, not really. Not the man who brought them presents from his travels, who sent them postcards and letters. Who sat with them so many nights by the fire, telling stories of the wonders he'd seen, while Dunne sat beside him, nodding and laughing.

Had Dunne and Sylvester done the same, for whoever owned those trunks of clothes?

"I have an idea," Henry said.

CHAPTER 17

HENRY SWALLOWED convulsively as all eyes turned to him. For a moment, he regretted even speaking. Of all his ideas since coming here, the Franklin bells was the only one to really work as he'd hoped.

Vincent met his gaze steadily. "Go on, Henry."

"It might not work." Henry realized he was twisting his hands together and forced them to still. "Seeing the equipment here made me think of it, but—"

"Get to the point, man!" Emberey exclaimed.

"Er, yes." Henry straightened. "Ghosts are weakened by sunlight, for reasons we don't entirely understand. Candles and gas don't seem to affect them, at least not all that much, nor does the reflected light of the sun from the face of the moon."

"We don't have time for a lecture, Henry," Lizzie warned.

"When we were in the cemetery, I thought I noticed Jo's head lamp drive Rosanna back a step. But Ortensi threw salt on her at the same time, and I assumed I'd been wrong." He gestured to the steam engine and dynamo. "But what if I wasn't? The arc lamp works on a different principle than a candle or gas lamp. If it affects the ghosts, even for a brief period, it might give us the opportunity to wrest the jar from Ortensi."

Emberey blinked. "Do you mean to say, if the moon tower had been repaired…"

"You might have had a great deal less trouble from Rosanna, yes. Er, possibly." Henry winced. "I don't know for sure. It might not work. Or I might not even be able to repair it."

"Anything is better than waiting for the ghosts to break in and kill us all," Vincent said. "Do it."

Henry swallowed again. "All right. Mr. Emberey, do you know what precisely broke on the moon tower?"

Emberey's brows knit together. "I believe the fellow said something about a feeder?"

"The automatic feeder?" Oh no.

"Yes, that was it."

"Blast."

"What is it?" Vincent asked, looking alarmed. "You can't fix it?"

"I won't know until I see it." Henry lifted his gaze to the shadowy interior of the tower. "The automatic feeder is a part of the lamp itself. To do any kind of repair, I'll have to go to the roof, then climb up onto the moon tower as well."

"Here," said Jo, digging into the satchel. "Take the headlamp so you can climb with both your hands free."

"Good idea, Jo." Henry took it from her. While she dumped tools and wire into the satchel, he struggled into the heavy pack holding the batteries. Vincent helped him with it, stepping back a pace when Henry pulled on the headband. The arc lamp, small as it was, sat heavily on his brow, and the strap of the weighty pack bit into his aching left shoulder. He'd exercised the limb far too much in the last few days, and once again he cursed Bamforth for shooting him at Reyhome.

"All right," he said. "Jo—"

"Look out!" shouted Lizzie from her station near the window.

Rosanna's shriek cut through the air. Every window facing the square exploded inward, glass showering the floor and mingling with the salt on the sills. The air instantly went frigid, and the light of their lanterns shaded to blue.

Henry rose from where he'd dropped to the floor. "Jo! Get the boiler going. As soon as the steam builds to a head, switch on the dynamo."

Worry creased her face. "But the wires will be live—if you're not done, you'll be electrocuted!"

"We don't have any more time." He glanced overhead, where the interior arc lamps lay dark. "If this works, you'll know in an instant. Even if I don't get the moon tower repaired in time, this will at least weaken any ghosts inside the building."

He turned to the stairs, as Jo opened the coal bin beside the furnace. Vincent seized his arm, halting him. Their eyes met, longing and fear in Vincent's gaze. No doubt it was reflected in his own. Had Emberey not been there, he would have flung his arms around Vincent and kissed him hard. But he couldn't, so he only said, "I'll be back soon."

Vincent's fingers tightened. "Don't get yourself electrocuted, Henry."

"I'll do my best," he replied. Then he pulled free and ran for the stairs.

Vincent turned away, the sound of Henry's shoes on the metal grate of the stairs ringing from above. He desperately wanted to go with Henry, as though his presence might afford his love some protection against all the things that might go wrong. The image of Henry plummeting from the moon tower presented itself, followed by Henry being electrocuted, or—

No. Henry counted on him to keep watch down here and make certain the ghosts remained on their side of the barrier. He strode back to the center of the room. "Mr. Emberey, start shoveling coal," he ordered.

Emberey drew himself up. "Shovel coal? The girl—"

"*The girl* is going to make sure this—" Vincent gestured at the steam engine and—what had Henry called it? A dynamo? "—works. Unless you have the knowledge to do the same, or have suddenly developed mediumistic talents, the best thing you can do is shovel coal and tend the furnace."

Orange light grew brighter in the window nearest the door, spilling inside as Rosanna drew closer. She hovered on the other side of the salt line, her flaming hair surrounding her burnt face like a corona.

Emberey's eyes went round. "I...yes," he said, and all but sprinted for the shovel.

"*Bring him back,*" Rosanna said, her voice like drops of water boiling off a hot griddle.

"We're trying," Vincent snapped.

The ghost began to pace, making her way along the row of broken windows. Seeking entrance. The wooden edges of the window frames scorched black beneath her heat, and the scent of burning wood mingled with the foul taste on his tongue.

"What is she doing?" he asked Lizzie.

"More importantly, what is Sylvester doing?" she replied.

His heart thumped in his throat. A quick look into the square outside showed it to be empty.

"That's not good," he said.

"Maybe he left." Lizzie's eyes tracked Rosanna's progress. "He realized he couldn't really go through with it."

The hope in her voice echoed Vincent's own. What if she was right, and Sylvester's conscience had awoken once again? What if Sylvester had found he could never really hurt them after all?

Rosanna screamed.

The windows on the side of the building burst inward. Jo let out a startled cry, and everyone ducked automatically, even though the glass didn't reach them.

There came the sound of splashing water.

Confused, Vincent raised his head. Sylvester stood framed in the window by the doorway, an empty bucket in his hands. Water pooled on the sill and ran down the inside of the wall, washing away the line of salt.

"No," Vincent whispered.

Sylvester stepped back. And the ghosts came pouring in.

The iron stairs and catwalk rang beneath Henry's shoes as he raced up the interior of the tower. He'd switched on the headlamp, and it burned like a miniature sun, sending rivulets of sweat down his face. The curved reflector directed its beam in front of him, sweeping across gears and counterweights, giving him brief glimpses of the clock's interior workings. The great pendulum swung past, and gears creaked. One of the hands lurched forward with a loud "tock."

The satchel of tools banged against his hip, clanking loudly, and the heavy batteries strapped to his back weighed him down. Before long, his legs ached and his lungs felt starved. He paused to catch his breath, straining to hear any sound that might tell him how the others fared below. Only silence greeted him; either he was too far away, or the salt lines yet held.

But for how long? Gritting his teeth, he jogged up the next flight of stairs.

At the top of the metal stairs lay a short ladder and a trap door. He flung open the trap door and emerged onto the small roof of the clock tower, gasping for breath. The metal scaffold of the moon tower rose another twenty feet into the air, the darkened arc lamp at the top.

A groan escaped him, and he rubbed his aching thighs. How long did he have until the pressure built up high enough to operate the steam engine?

Rosanna's scream echoed from below, and even at a distance every hair on his arms stood up. The sound of shattering glass accompanied the unearthly shriek, and his heart lurched. What was happening below? Was Jo safe? Vincent? Lizzie? Had Rosanna found a way inside?

They all depended on him, on this mad idea he'd proposed. What if it didn't work? What if he was as wrong about this as he'd been about everything else?

Shoving aside all his doubts, he reached for the first cross bar of the iron scaffolding comprising the moon tower. The ache of his left shoulder turned to stabbing pain as he hauled himself up. Henry gritted his teeth and silently prayed the shoulder didn't give out altogether. He had to reach the top and the arc lamp itself, no matter what.

There came a cry from somewhere far below. He glanced down automatically—and instantly wished he hadn't. The roofs of Devil's Walk stretched out below him, and moonlight frosted the forest. It was all a very, very long way down.

His hands froze on the iron beams, and his breath hitched. The world seemed to swim around him. He'd never had difficulty with heights before—but he'd never been up this far. It would take a long time to hit the ground if he fell from this distance.

"Move, Henry," he muttered to himself between clenched teeth. "You promised Vincent you wouldn't get electrocuted."

Forcing his fingers to unbend, he reached for the next iron beam.

The dead of Devil's Walk poured in through the broken window like floodwaters through a breached dam. Instantly the air went to ice, and even the hot glow of the furnace took on a sickly blue hue. Emberey cried out in terror and froze, his shovel lifted as though he meant to beat off the ghosts with it.

"Keep stoking!" Vincent shouted. God, they had to do something to protect Jo and Emberey long enough for them to get the steam engine running. The arc lights overhead would weaken the ghosts—assuming Henry's theory was correct—but they had to get electricity to them first.

Lizzie hurled handfuls of salt from one of the half-empty bags. It tore smoking holes through streaming ectoplasm, and the dead fell back, swirling in pain and confusion.

"Leave this place! Return to the otherworld!" she shouted.

Some of them vanished...but as experience had already shown, it would take nothing for Sylvester to bring them forth again.

Vincent cast about wildly—there had to be some way to hold them off. Henry's backpack lay abandoned where he'd left it, the tip of a copper rod protruding from the half open flap.

Vincent yanked it free; the rubber glove flopped out as well, caught amidst the tangle of wires. He'd used the ghost grounder once before, and knew the principles well enough. He just needed something to attach the wires too, something grounded. The bolts anchoring the dynamo to the floor caught his eye, and they were in a good position to let him protect Jo and Emberey.

"Vincent!" Lizzie shouted. "I'm almost out of salt!"

Curse it. He ran to the dynamo, ignoring Emberey's fearful yelp. Securing the wire to one of the bolts, he offered up a brief prayer this would indeed work.

A ghost darted past Lizzie and made for Emberey. Its eyes gleamed, sickly yellow corpse candles in the midst of roiling ectoplasm. Emberey screamed and cowered, dropping the shovel to the floor with a clatter. Vincent stabbed the tip of the ghost grounder deep into where the ghost's heart would have been, were it still alive.

There came a crackle, and it dissolved into nothingness.

"We're almost there!" called Jo. "Mr. Emberey, keep stoking!"

"We've got you," Vincent said. "Let Lizzie and I handle the ghosts. We won't allow them to get through."

They took up point, each facing a different direction. Vincent slashed and stabbed, sometimes dispelling the ghosts on contact, more often simply draining them bit by bit. At his back, Lizzie ordered the ghosts to return to the otherworld in a ringing voice, scattering salt as she did so.

It worked. The crowd of spirits around them thinned. The temperature crept back up to something, if not warm, at least not arctic. The ghosts Sylvester sent against them were no spirits of rage like Rosanna. These were ordinary people, who had passed peacefully and made only shadows when called back to this world.

So where had Rosanna gone?

"Vincent," Lizzie said in a low, urgent voice. "The door."

He glanced over his shoulder, and his heart sank as his question was answered.

The door lock glowed, first a sullen red, then brighter, edging into blinding yellow. "Rosanna's burning through the door," he said. "Jo! Is it ready?"

"Almost!"

"Almost isn't good enough!"

The lock and knob fell free in a molten glob onto the floor. The door hurled open, scattering salt everywhere.

Sylvester stood there, silhouetted against the burning houses on the other side of the square. His hazel eyes were hard, his hair in disarray. He spared a look for Vincent—and ran for the stairs.

No—he must have spotted Henry on top of the tower. Vincent shouted a denial and started to drop the ghost grounder.

"Don't." Lizzie grabbed his arm. "If you go after Sylvester, the ghosts will get past, and we'll all be lost."

He wanted to deny it. Wanted to leave anyway. To run to Henry's rescue, to scream at the top of his lungs that Sylvester was coming with murder in his eyes.

Instead, he firmed his grip on the ghost grounder and stabbed the nearest spirit through its glowing eye.

By the time Henry reached the top of the moon tower, he felt as though his head were baking and his left shoulder actively afire. The great arc lamp jutted up from the center of the scaffolding, cold and dark in the beam of his headlamp. The wind tore at his hair and clothing, like phantom hands trying to pull him from the tower.

At least they weren't real phantom hands. Not yet, anyway.

It wasn't something he could worry about at the moment. He linked one arm through the uppermost crossbar of the tower and peered at the automatic feeder. If the fault were in one of the electromagnetic coils, he'd never be able to repair it in time.

The headlamp might be hot as a coal strapped to his forehead, but the light it put out illuminated the mechanism perfectly. The coils seemed intact, and the carbon electrodes in place. What then…ah. There it was. The latch that regulated the coils had become misaligned somehow and jammed against them.

Now came the hard part—making the repair without toppling off the metal scaffolding to his death.

Henry shucked off his coat and slung it around his waist. The sleeves he tied together on the other side of the uppermost iron bar. With any luck, the makeshift sling would let him use both hands without falling backwards off the moon tower, even with the weight of the batteries on his back. The satchel he looped around his neck to hang in front of him. Its strap cut uncomfortably into the back of his neck, but he ignored it in favor of digging through for a small screwdriver. If he removed the latch and realigned it, the automatic feeder should work as intended.

How much time did he have left? How close was the engine below to full steam? If it was already running, could he still do the repair in any safety and dispel the ghosts in the square outside the building?

Putting aside questions to which he had no answer, he carefully set about unscrewing the latch. If he dropped it or the screw, they would have no hope of fixing the lamp. Ortensi would keep summoning ghosts. Even if the arc lamps came on inside the building, there was nothing to keep him from attacking the rest of Devil's Walk as a plot to force Vincent and Lizzie out into the open.

There. It was done. As soon as power was restored, the electromagnetic coils would feed the carbon electrodes into the correct position, and the lamp would burn again.

His hands shaking, Henry untied his coat and let it tumble free. Pain flared in his left shoulder with every movement, but he slowly, slowly climbed down. He kept his attention on the iron cross beams directly in front of him, careful not to look down. His legs ached, and his left hand didn't grip as it should, but he finally reached the roof. With a groan, he leaned against the tower, his whole body trembling. He wanted nothing but to collapse.

But there was still no light. Had something gone wrong below? The breaking glass he'd heard—had the ghosts somehow gained entrance? If they'd hurt Jo…

Stifling another moan at the pain in his limbs, he pushed himself off the tower and turned. Ortensi stood between him and the trap door.

CHAPTER 18

HENRY'S HEART pounded from a mixture of exertion and fear. Ortensi stood before him, coat flapping in the wind. In his hand he held the small earthenware jar.

Oh God. If Ortensi was here, the defenses below must be breached. What had happened to Jo, to Vincent? Did they still live?

Ortensi paced forward, his hazel eyes fixed on Henry. "Well, well. I underestimated you, Mr. Strauss," he said, as if they'd met on a street corner and not atop a tower with the wind screaming around them and ghosts screaming below. "I viewed you as a threat. A part of the new order, determined to sweep relics such as myself under the rug. To forget the old ways, the old powers." A small smile touched his mouth. "I dismissed the sentiment when Vincent said James would have loved you, but perhaps I was wrong."

Henry tried to back up, but his shoulders collided with the tower. Sweat slicked his palms and the headlamp felt like a miniature sun strapped to his forehead. "What do you mean?" he asked.

"I should have offered to join forces, rather than try to discredit you." Ortensi gave Henry an assessing look. "I forgot what James always knew—how to select the right tool for the right job. I need money to travel, fame to gain access to the last pieces of knowledge we need. Money and fame, the very things you crave most of all, but haven't attained on your own."

Ortensi lifted the jar, as if Henry might have missed it. "With this simple object, my return to the stage is secured. But your inventions would give my séances a modern flair. Few doors would remain closed to us." A fatherly smile crept across his face. "You wish to provide for your cousin, do you not? Imagine what an education at the finest universities of Europe might do for her. Here, she'll be lucky to find a negro college that accepts women, let alone prepares them to be anything more than teachers or nurses. Your dreams for yourself will be assured, and you'll never have to worry for her again. What do you say?"

Some mad part of Henry wanted to laugh. If someone had asked him this a year ago, if he'd stood here, having never met Vincent, the answer would have been obvious. Easy. "Vincent will never stand for it."

Ortensi snorted scornfully. "That is where you're wrong, my friend. James didn't choose Lizzie and Vincent for their independent spirits. He knew that just a little bit of kindness, the sort of decency most of us take for granted, would gain their blind devotion. They would have cut off their own hands if he'd asked." Sadness flashed over Ortensi's face. "James's death was hard on all of us. If I'd been able to return immediately and take his place in their lives, perhaps there would have been no disruption. No chance for them to consider anything else. It will take time, but I can still earn back Vincent's loyalty and trust, even if Lizzie is a lost cause. *If* you help me."

Henry's hands felt cold despite the sweat dripping from his brow. "You want me to convince Vincent to listen to you. To go along with your plans, with your use of a necromantic artifact."

"The rewards for you will be great." Ortensi's smile took on an edge of triumph. "With my name and the power of this jar behind us, we'll perform before Queen Victoria herself. I'll be able to do what none other truly has and summon her lost Albert back to her, under the guise of using your machines. Your devices will divert any suspicion of my sudden talent, and gain you international acclaim. The Psychical Society will be sorry they ever turned you away. They'll beg for your forgiveness."

Henry's stomach rolled, the same way it had in the forest, when he'd turned over the old sign and found the writhing maggots underneath. Whatever Ortensi might have been, whatever scheme he and Dunne had supposedly concocted, there was nothing but a kindly veneer masking corruption.

"Go to hell," Henry growled.

Ortensi's smile dissolved. "Have it your way, Mr. Strauss," he snarled.

Rosanna flamed into being behind him.

Vincent's wrist ached from holding the ghost grounder, and yet the spirits kept coming. Whatever power the jar had given Fitzwilliam to command, it was nothing as compared to its potential in the hands of a true medium. No wonder Sylvester spoke so admiringly about Rosanna's ability, to have created something like this.

Thank God for the ghost grounder. The mediums' commands might not be able to overcome the power of the jar, but the grounder still worked as it always did. Every bit of energy it stole from the ghosts offered them another few seconds of life.

Had Sylvester reached Henry yet? Would he attack Henry with the knife, or merely summon more ghosts to him? Or...

Oh no. Rosanna had vanished after opening the door. But Sylvester surely hadn't let her go. She'd burn Henry, turn him into a pillar of flame like Fitzwilliam. And all the while Vincent was trapped down here, desperately trying to save everyone else, while the man he loved screamed and died.

"I'm out of salt," Lizzie said, and flung the empty bag at one of the ghosts. It went through his insubstantial body and struck the floor.

"Can we run for it?" Emberey asked. "While Ortensi is occupied?"

"No." Lizzie backed rapidly toward the dynamo. "There are other ghosts outside, waiting in the square. This is our only chance."

"Get behind me, Lizzie," Vincent ordered. He slashed at a ghost coalescing beside her, leaving his other flank exposed.

Emberey screamed as unseen hands yanked him away from the furnace. His shovel scraped along the floor. He swung it frantically. The iron made contact, and the hands dragging him let go. But before he could scramble back, more grabbed him. He flew into the wall, and there came a snap as his arm broke against the brick, accompanied by his cry of agony.

Vincent yelled. He to had get to Emberey, and protect Jo and Lizzie at the same time, but how?

A powerful blow struck his back.

"Vincent!" Lizzie shouted.

He stabbed blindly about him with the ghost grounder, but at least one spirit had learned to avoid it. Another blow struck him on the side, then on the knee. He went to the floor, curling to protect his vitals as unseen hands pummeled him. "Jo!" he shouted.

"It's ready!" she yelled. "Shield your eyes!"

The lights overhead blazed to life.

Henry flung up his hands, as if the gesture would somehow hold the ghost back. "No—don't!"

"End him," Ortensi ordered.

The light of Henry's miniature arc lamp fell across Rosanna's face. Her image seemed to thin, her movements stutter.

He'd been right. The miniature arc lamp did affect her. Just not enough to stop her.

She stalked toward him, compelled no matter what he did to her. As long as Ortensi held the jar, its necromantic power would force her to obey his will.

It was impossible to see if any regret lived in her blank, boiled eyes. Her hair burned in a fiery cloud around her face. Blackened skin cracked on her cheeks as her mouth opened, revealing fire-shattered teeth.

Henry backed up, trying to put as much distance between them as possible. But the top of the clock tower was small, and made even more cramped by the moon tower and its guy wires. The edge of the roof stopped him far too soon.

Ice cold air caressed his face as she stalked closer. But it wouldn't stay cold for long. In a few moments, she'd incinerate him, as surely as she had Fitzwilliam. Desperate to slow her, even for a moment, Henry snatched tools from the satchel hanging in front of him and flung them at the ghost. The brass ones had no effect, but she snarled and jerked back from an iron wrench. A hole tore in her ectoplasm, and she growled when the beam of his arc lamp crossed the wound.

But she still didn't stop.

"No," he said, crouching at the very edge of the roof, even though he knew the words would do no good. "Please, Rosanna, stop, stop!"

She came to a halt only inches from him. The intense cold began to reverse itself. Heat poured out of her, the suddenly hot air creating a breeze against Henry's cheek, lifting the edge of his hair.

Rosanna stretched out a hand. Henry found himself staring fixedly at the broken nails, the bloody, blackened skin as it moved closer and closer. One touch, and he'd die as she had, his body wreathed in flame.

"Please," he whispered.

"You should have taken my offer, Mr. Strauss," Ortensi said. "There's no one here to save you."

The great arc lamp overhead blazed to life.

Rosanna arched back, her mouth stretched into a silent scream. The light struck her like a strong wind scattering ash, bits of burned skin and hair flaking away, first a few, then more and more. At the same moment, she grew fainter, less substantial—until with a faint pop, she vanished into nothingness.

Henry sat back on his heels, gasping. His heart felt as though it might burst from his chest, and all his limbs turned to water. Blinking against the harsh light of the great lamp, he stumbled to his feet and looked up.

Just in time to see Ortensi rushing toward him.

There was no time to dodge, no time even to think. Ortensi's hands slammed into his chest, and Henry fell. His hip hit the edge of the roof, and he grabbed wildly at the bricks, a scream of terror torn from his throat. His elbow collided with one of the guy wires anchored to the roof's corner, and he seized it instinctively, even as his legs slid over the edge.

Agony shot through his left shoulder, and he nearly lost his grip on the wire before he managed to seize it with his right hand as well. It helped—but not by much. All of his weight plus the batteries dragged him down, the straps of the pack cutting into his shoulders. How long could he hope to hold onto the wire, before his aching fingers slipped and sent him to his death?

Ortensi loomed up, his shadow falling over Henry. "You have the devil's own luck," he snarled. "But it ends here."

"Sylvester!" Vincent shouted. "Get away from him!"

The effect was instantaneous. Arc lamps blazed overhead, as the dynamo spun to life. The sludgy taste in Vincent's mouth vanished, and ectoplasm dissolved beneath the onslaught of the artificial illumination. Harsh, white light showed through the windows as well, competing with the flames to illuminate the square.

Lizzie shaded her eyes. "No wonder Emberey didn't want this glaring through his window," she said, even as she hurried to the man's side. Emberey groaned and whimpered, clutching at his arm, but seemed otherwise unhurt.

"It worked!" Jo exclaimed, eyes bright with excitement. "Just like Henry said."

Henry.

Vincent dropped the ghost grounder and ran for the stairs. "Keep an eye on Jo and Emberey, Lizzie," he called. "Just in case something goes wrong and we lose the light."

The steel stairs rang under his feet as he bolted for the roof. His legs ached, as did the rest of his body, but he didn't even feel the pain through his terror for Henry.

The glare of the arc lamp shone down through an open trap door. He was almost there—just a short ladder between him and the rooftop.

Henry's scream cut through the air.

Vincent didn't remember climbing the ladder; it seemed the next instant he dragged himself onto the roof. The harsh light of the arc lamp seemed to pick out every detail of the scene, even the smallest irregularities of the bricks outlined in sharp-edged shadows. Henry's tools lay scattered across the roof, as if flung by a careless hand. Sylvester stood at the edge of the tower, his back to Vincent. But where was Henry?

Sylvester. The edge of the tower. Had Henry screamed as he fell to his death?

Vincent's heart seemed to stutter in his chest. The world froze, dipped in cold treacle, and his pulse turned sluggish.

The beam of a much smaller arc lamp flashed across the edge of the tower, in Sylvester's shadow. Henry clung to one of the guy wires strung from the moon tower to the roof corners. He was alive.

And Sylvester meant to kill him.

"Sylvester!" Vincent shouted. "Get away from him!"

Sylvester turned, even as Vincent reached him. Before the other medium reacted, Vincent grabbed him by the coat and shoved him hard into the moon tower.

The older man struck the iron with bruising force. The necromantic jar tumbled from his grip, hit the ground, and rolled away intact.

"Vincent!" Henry shouted.

"I'm here!" He started for Henry.

Then Sylvester was on him. A hard arm wrapped around his neck, jerking him back and nearly off his feet. Vincent clawed at Sylvester's arm, but his grip was like an iron bar against Vincent's throat, cutting off his air.

"There was no need for this," Sylvester growled in his ear. "No need for any of this! If you'd only listened, your Mr. Strauss would be safe, and you and Lizzie would be leaving here on the morning train with me. Instead you're determined to destroy everything. I should have realized James made a mistake in choosing you. After all, it's your fault he's dead."

Vincent snapped his head back with all his strength. His skull collided with Sylvester's face, already tender from the blow Fitzwilliam had dealt him.

Sylvester let out a bellow and his hold loosened. Vincent tore free and stumbled forward, gasping for breath. His shin collided with the base of the moon tower. He fell onto the bricks, scraping his palms raw against them. One of the scattered tools, an iron wrench, clattered away from his fingers.

Out of the corner of his eye, he saw Sylvester's calfskin shoes, now stained with mud and dust, crossing the roof toward Henry.

"Vincent!" Henry shouted. "I can't hold on much longer!"

Vincent's hand closed on the iron wrench. Lunging to his feet, he flung it into the arc lamp.

Something burst in a shower of sparks, plunging the world into darkness, save for the beam from Henry's headlamp. Vincent groped in the direction he'd last seen the small earthenware jar.

Sylvester shouted for him to stop, but Vincent reached the jar first. His hands closed around the cool surface—

Power trembled on his tongue, buzzed beneath his skin, like a thousand angry hornets. He sensed the spirits of the dead like never before, scattered throughout Devil's Walk, or else watching through the veil from the otherworld. Each individual flavor, with a hundred nuances that somehow communicated far more to him than simple taste should.

But he wanted only a single spirit, and his awareness of her burned as if he'd swallowed a live coal.

"I summon you, spirit of Rosanna!" he shouted, lifting the jar high.

She burst into being, between him and Sylvester. And with all the strength left in his arms, he brought the jar binding her down onto the bricks.

The pottery exploded into fragments, releasing iron nails and dust, red hair and a scrap of cloth, and something which looked suspiciously like a tiny piece of leather, long desiccated.

"You're free," he said aloud. "You're all free."

"No!" shouted Sylvester. "You fool! What...no. Stay back!"

The last was directed at Rosanna. Her raw, bare feet paced across the brick, her dress trailing fire. Her mouth split into a horrible grin, revealing fire-blackened teeth and the charred stump of a tongue.

"I command you," Sylvester began.

He never finished. Between one second and the next, she was on him.

Vincent didn't look—the screams were bad enough. Instead, he ran across the roof, to where Henry still hung from the guy wire. "I'm here," he said, dropping to his knees.

Henry's eyes were wide with terror. "I can't—" Henry said.

His left hand slipped free.

Vincent seized the straps of the pack holding the batteries, hooking his fingers beneath them. "I've got you," he gasped, even though the muscles in his shoulders and back screamed. "Pull yourself up, if you can."

He flung all his weight backward. Henry's right hand still gripped the guy wire, and he let out a whimper as he used it to haul himself onto the roof. A few seconds later, Vincent toppled back onto the brick, Henry tumbling onto him after.

"Oh God." Henry shook, whether from fear or pain or both, Vincent didn't know. He pulled the headlamp from Henry's forehead and set it aside, then wrapped his arms tight around his lover.

"It's all right," he said. "It's all right, sweetheart. I've got you, and I'm not letting go. Not ever."

Flames flickered on the other side of the tower, but they had already died into nothingness around the contorted, blackened thing, which was all that remained of Sylvester. Of Rosanna there was no trace.

"It worked," Henry said. "Did you see, Vincent? My idea worked."

Vincent laughed, despite everything. "I saw." He cupped Henry's face in his hands. "My clever, clever love."

There came the sound of footsteps echoing from below. "Vincent? Henry?" Lizzie called. "The ghosts are gone. Are you still alive up there?"

Vincent sighed and let go of Henry reluctantly. "Come on," he said. "Before Mr. Emberey puts in an appearance and finds us in a compromising position. After all this, I'd hate not to get paid."

CHAPTER 19

"ARE YOU sure it was smart to wait until sundown to do this?" Henry asked.

He and Vincent stood in the midst of the small clearing where they'd found Norris's body only a few days earlier. Whether it had any special meaning to Rosanna, neither of them knew, but at least it was some distance from the construction. Hopefully what they meant to bury there would remain undisturbed.

"I'm sure," Vincent said. He leaned on a shovel and wiped the sweat from his brow. Henry had started to dig the hole, but his left shoulder remained a mass of dull pain. After watching Henry's awkward attempts with the shovel, Vincent took it from him and ordered him to stand aside. "I think this is deep enough."

Henry took a small wooden box from his coat pocket. Within lay what resembled a scrap of dried leather—all that remained of a tiny heart. "I don't know whether to feel sorry for Rosanna or not," he confessed. "She suffered at the hands of her community, first when they rejected her baby, and again when they burned her alive. But she murdered Zadock and enslaved a spirit to do her bidding, just as she herself was later enslaved."

"I know." Vincent's mouth quirked into a slight frown. "But it doesn't really matter what we feel. We have a job to do."

"Yes. You're quite right." Henry knelt and placed the box in the hole. When he was done, Vincent shoveled earth on top of it.

"There." Vincent patted the last of the loose dirt into place. Handing the shovel to Henry, he tipped his head back and addressed the woods. "We've done as you asked. We've brought your son back to you."

The sensation of being watched crept over Henry's skin. "Is she here?" he murmured.

Vincent nodded, but didn't look at Henry. Instead he kept his eyes fixed on some indeterminate point amidst the trees. "Spirit of Rosanna, your child is at rest. The necromantic jar you created is shattered. Your time in this world ended long ago."

A light appeared among the trees. Henry let out a gasp. "Vincent, be careful!"

The light drew closer and closer, until Rosanna stood before them. Fire wreathed her face, and her blank eyes fixed on them. Henry locked his knees against the urge to grab Vincent and flee.

Vincent, on the other hand, didn't seem afraid at all. "Rosanna," he said, and his voice was gentle even though it still rang with authority. "It's time for you to rest. To join your child's spirit in the otherworld."

The flames faded, leaving behind only a young woman, not much older than Jo. Her red hair fell around her shoulders, and her green eyes shone with an inner light, set in a pale face whose skin was untouched by flame.

"Go," Vincent said.

She reached out to him with pale fingers. But as her hand drew closer to him, it became less and less substantial, until her entire being dissolved into nothingness.

For a long moment, the woods around them remained silent. Then a cricket let out a tentative chirp. Soon others of its kind followed suit, until the forest seemed alive in a way it hadn't before.

"Well, that's it," Vincent said with a weary smile.

They made their way back to the rail spur, hands linked. Within a few days, the area would again be a hive of activity, as soon as Emberey's replacement workers arrived from Pittsburgh. But for now it was peaceful, the woods still in the silver moonlight.

"I can't wait to get back to Baltimore," Vincent said as they walked. "I've come to the conclusion that all of this country air is terrible for one's health."

Henry snorted. "I imagine country air doesn't ordinarily come laden with murderous spirits."

"Perhaps, but best not to risk it."

It got a short laugh out of Henry. The sound echoed, startling the crickets into silence for a few seconds. Uncertain whether he should bring up the subject or not, Henry said, "I'm sorry about Ortensi."

Vincent kept his eyes focused on the railroad tracks unspooling before them. "So am I."

"The things he said to you about Dunne...I'm sure he lied," Henry offered. "He meant to convince you to join him in the only way he knew."

"Perhaps." Vincent shook his head. "I let the past blind me to the present. I should never have listened to the things he said about you, about my place in your life. Instead, I blindly followed his lead, just as I would have Dunne's."

"I certainly didn't help things," Henry said, squeezing Vincent's fingers. "I know you've forgiven me, but I still feel stupid for lying to you. I was a fool."

"No argument there."

"Beast." Henry swatted at him.

Vincent jumped away with a laugh. But after a moment, his grin wavered. "Will you be honest with me?"

"I'll never lie to you again." What oath would be weighty enough to convince Vincent of his sincerity? "I swear it on my father's grave."

Vincent bowed his head slightly in acknowledgment. "Without your ghost grounder, we would have died a dozen times over last night. Even then, I couldn't have held the summoned spirits off forever. Your idea to use the arc lamps against the ghosts saved all our lives, and kept Sylvester from escaping with the jar."

Henry flushed, although in truth the words pleased him. "It was nothing."

"It was everything." Vincent stopped, forcing Henry to as well. "You're a great thinker, Henry. An innovator. You have so much to offer the world. Tell me truthfully...even if the answer isn't what I want to hear...do you regret going into business with Lizzie and me? I know a small shop with modest clientele was never your dream. I know you can do better. If you feel we're holding you back—"

Henry pulled Vincent to him, and silenced him with a kiss. "There is your answer," Henry said, when he could speak again. "But if it isn't clear enough, allow me to say...I love you, Vincent Night. You and Jo are the most important things in the world to me. No amount of acclaim would mean anything without you to share in it."

Vincent's smile was brighter than the moon, more blinding than the arc lamp. "I love you, too, Henry. More than I can say."

Henry's heart felt too big for words, so he hugged Vincent close. They rested against one another, arms loose around each other's waists. Henry took a deep breath, the familiar citrus and musk of Vincent's cologne like a balm to nerves fractured from the last few days.

He would have been content to stay like that forever. But of course it wasn't possible. Vincent stole another kiss, then reluctantly pulled free. "We should return to the hotel before anyone comes looking for us. I expect Lizzie and Jo are even now convincing themselves something went horribly wrong with Rosanna. They'll set out to rescue us if we linger any more."

"You're probably right." Henry picked up the shovel and rested it against his right shoulder. The left still hurt, and he hoped he hadn't managed to injure it even further somehow. As they started to walk again, he said, "I've been thinking."

"Always a perilous undertaking."

"Oh, ha ha. With such a wit, you should be the one touring the world."

Vincent bumped him lightly with his hip. "I've always thought my true talents were wasted."

"*If* I may continue," Henry said with a scowl. "There is a space above my workshop in the back that could be converted into a small apartment. No one would think anything about it if one of the owners of our business moved into it. And no, before you make some clever remark, I'm not talking about Lizzie."

Vincent's dark eyes widened. "What are you saying?"

Henry shrugged, suddenly uncomfortable. "I'm saying I want to be with you. On a daily basis. I'd still have my room above the store itself, of course, but I think we could make the workshop into a comfortable little home. It would give us a bit more privacy, and, well..." he trailed off. "Of course you'll need time to think about it, and if you say no, I completely—"

"Yes."

Henry stopped walking. "You will?"

Vincent grinned down at him. "Yes. It's a brilliant idea. I want to go to sleep with you every night, and wake up with you every morning."

Henry felt as though gravity had stopped working, and he might fly off above the trees at any second. "It will take some effort to get it ready."

Vincent leaned down and kissed him. "I know. But you're worth it."

He laced his fingers together with Henry's. Hand in hand, they walked down the tracks out of the forest and into the clear light of the moon.

ABOUT THE AUTHOR

Jordan L. Hawk is a trans author from North Carolina. Childhood tales of mountain ghosts and mysterious creatures gave him a life-long love of things that go bump in the night. When he isn't writing, he brews his own beer and tries to keep the cats from destroying the house. His best-selling Whyborne & Griffin series (beginning with *Widdershins*) can be found in print, ebook, and audiobook.

If you're interested in receiving Jordan's newsletter and being the first to know when new books are released, please sign up at his website: jordanlhawk.com.

Made in the USA
Middletown, DE
20 September 2021